GILBERT MORRIS AND BOBBY FUNDERBURK

A TIME TO HEAL

WORD PUBLISHING

Dallas · London · Vancouver · Melbourne

Library of Congress Cataloging-in-Publication Data

Morris, Gilbert.
    A time to heal / Gilbert Morris and Bobby Funderburk.
        p.   cm. — (Price of liberty series: #6)
    ISBN 0–8499–3512–1
    1. World War, 1939–1945—Fiction.   I. Funderburk, Bobby, 1942–   . II. Title.   III. Series: Morris, Gilbert. Price of liberty ; 6.
    PS3563.08742T565   1994
    813'.54—dc20   94–27309
                                                              CIP

Printed in the United States of America

456789 LB 987654321

To Jeannette Troescher, my sister-in-law,
Whose gentle spirit puts me in mind of a passage
from Paul's second letter to Timothy: "And the
servant of the Lord must not strive;
but be gentle unto all men."

Bobby

CONTENTS

Part 1

THE GOOD AND GENTLE NIGHTS

1

THE CRACK OF THE BAT

Clayton McCain would never forget that day in early April 1942 when Ted Williams came to Liberty, Georgia. It was a time when sunlight, as gold as freshly churned butter, poured down warmly on the tender spring grass of the outfield and on the dusty pitcher's mound as Clay walked toward it from the bullpen where he had rocked the second-string catcher back on his heels with his fastball; a time when Diane Jackson, whose soft auburn hair and green eyes he loved even more than baseball, couldn't bear to be apart from him. It was a time when he woke each morning full of life and slept untroubled through the good and gentle nights, as yet untouched by the random butchery of war.

Breathing deeply the heady perfume of the sweet olive trees planted in precise rows along the fences, Clay glanced toward the stands, and there he was! Ted Williams, the man who had become the premier player in baseball at the age of twenty-four, actually sat behind home plate in the ballpark at Liberty High School. He had hit .406 for the Red Sox in '41, and everyone in the sporting world felt that he would probably be the last man to have a four-hundred season.

Oh, Lord! How am I ever gonna pitch this game with Ted Williams watching me? Clay brushed a lock of light brown hair back from his face, leaned his rangy six-foot-three-inch frame over, and picked up the rosin bag. Taking a deep breath, he closed his eyes. Letting his breath out slowly, he thought, *Well, big league baseball's all about how a man can handle pressure. I reckon this is as good a time as any to see if I can pitch when I'm under the gun. Just throw 'em like I was practicing with that old tire in the back yard and let the hair go with the hide.*

In the bleachers, J.T. Dickerson, sipping from a bottle of Coke liberally laced with moonshine, sat next to his longtime friend,

Benny Risemer, a scout for the Red Sox. J.T. had dressed to the nines for the occasion, which meant he had put on his cleanest dirty shirt and most unwrinkled sport coat, and had scraped most of the dried mud from the soles of his shoes.

J.T. had also shaved and had almost washed his thick brown hair, but he decided that slicking it down with a few drops of Wildroot Hair Tonic would suffice. "How about it, Mr. Williams? You think we've got another Bob Feller out there on the mound?"

Williams, in his brown sport coat and open-collar shirt a taller, cleaner, younger version of J.T., sat on the other side of Risemer. "There's only *one* Bob Feller, J.T. Let's wait and see how he handles this game. He knows we're up here watching him now. And I wish you'd stop calling me *Mister* Williams. I'm young enough to be your son."

J.T. took a pull from his Coke bottle. "Anybody that swings a bat the way you do is *Mister* to me. One day a quarter of a century from now I'll be telling the boys in the War Veterans' home how I sat on the bleachers one beautiful spring day with the great Ted Williams."

Smiling, Williams shook his head and gazed out at Clay who was throwing the last of his warmup pitches. He took note of the young pitcher's smooth, effortless motion that was either a part of a man or not—it could not be learned.

J.T. glanced down at the growing pile of peanut shells at Risemer's feet. "What do you think, Benny?"

"I think the best thing that ever happened to me was not letting you talk me into staying in law school when we were at Harvard. I got to play ten years at shortstop and then landed this scouting job, which is almost as much fun as playing. That's what I think." Risemer brushed his hands on the pants of his gray suit, slick with wear from his dozens of train trips to high schools around the country scouting prospects for the Red Sox.

"You just can't help some people, I guess," J.T. retorted. "Here you are bumming around the country when you could be a prosperous and respected counselor like me."

Remembering the promising future J.T. had during their years at Harvard, Risemer smiled almost sadly at his old friend. "I think the second best thing that ever happened to me was letting you talk me into coming down here to see this kid, McCain. He'll go down in the record books if he can hold it together up here." Risemer tapped his right temple with a stubby forefinger.

"He can," J.T. offered with conviction. "He's had a lot of practice at getting mentally tough. Comes from good solid stock, but his folks don't have much money, so he's had to help pay his own way. He's worked at the *Liberty Herald* the whole time he's been in high school."

"Maybe he's got guts enough to make it in the pro's then," Risemer agreed. "Talent doesn't mean a thing without a whole lot of tenacity to go along with it."

"That was a great idea—calling Williams in on the deal." J.T. turned the Coke bottle up again. "How did you talk him into coming down here?"

"Fishing."

"Fishing?"

"Sure, he loves it. I just told him some of those fish stories you've been boring me to death with for years—you know, about those fifteen-pound bass in the lake outside of town—and he decided he could spare two days away from spring training if he could get a crack at one that size."

"Biggest one I ever heard of weighed eleven pounds, Benny. I told you that."

Risemer gave him a wry smile. "What's four pounds among friends?"

J.T. chuckled softly and took another quick swallow from his bottle.

Risemer took off his gray fedora and wiped his bald head with a red handkerchief, glancing at J.T.'s bottle. "You ought to ease off on that stuff. Your liver's probably the size of that catcher's mitt down there."

J.T. held the bottle up in front of him; the sunlight gleamed faintly through the dark liquid. "Closest thing I've got to a wife, Benny. Got to be faithful to her."

"What you need is a divorce. You're a lawyer—or so you tell me. Handle it yourself." Risemer frowned. "Have the Yankees been back in touch with your boy yet?"

"Not as far as I know." J.T. pictured himself in a courtroom arguing for a divorce from his whiskey bottle. "Your Honor, the defendant and I have irreconcilable differences," he would say, pointing to the bottle in the witness chair.

"Good. I think Ted can swing the deal for us," Risemer mumbled, popping peanuts into his mouth. "What kid could turn down the greatest hitter in baseball?"

J.T. glanced over at Williams. "Let's just hope they don't bring DiMaggio down here before we get Clay signed up. I'd hate to see him playing with the Yankees."

"Don't even think about it," Risemer grimaced. "DiMaggio at the plate and McCain on the mound for the Yankees. They'd have the Series wrapped up for the next decade."

"You really think he's that good?"

"I think he's that good," Risemer nodded sagely. "What do you think, Ted?"

"With two years experience he could be the hottest pitcher in the game." Williams leaned forward and watched Clay blaze a fastball past the batter for strike three. "If I'm any judge at all, that fastball's already better than ninety miles an hour. All he needs now is a little more control and a couple of years to fill out and build up some more strength and stamina."

Settling back with his arms resting on the seat behind him, J.T. breathed the mild, flower-scented air deeply into his lungs. The liquor coursed darkly through his brain as it always did when he took his first drinks of the day, giving him a sense of warmth and well-being.

The first baseman caught a high pop fly to put out the third batter. J.T. gazed down at Liberty's rising star as he walked back to the dugout from the pitcher's mound. Thinking back over the years that he had known Clay, he felt a private sense of accomplishment. After all, he *had* been the first one to show the boy, eight years old at the time, how to pitch a baseball and had given him pointers on his game until he made the high school varsity squad at the age of fourteen. *I threw away my shot at pro football. Maybe I'll get to watch Clay make it big in baseball. Wouldn't that be great?*

For the rest of the game, J.T. let himself slide into reveries of the past, talking little with Risemer and Williams as he sipped from his Coke bottle, refilling it from time to time from a silver flask he carried in his jacket pocket. He remembered the years when Clay had done yard work at his office and his house, until he had sold it and started living at the office as his law practice began dissolving in alcohol.

14

Dobe Jackson had given Clay a job at his newspaper, the *Liberty Herald*, at J.T.'s request. This had not only helped Clay and his family financially but had also put him in close proximity to Dobe's daughter, Diane, and the two of them had been virtually inseparable for the last two years.

J.T. had seldom missed one of Clay's games, even the ones out of town. He thought of himself as a kind of father by proxy since Hartley Lambert, who owned the lumber mill where Clay's father worked, never let his employees off before six o'clock unless someone in the family died.

Lost in these and many more memories, J.T. snapped back to the present when a cheer went up from the crowd at the end of the game.

* * *

"Oh, Clay, you're the best baseball player in the country." Diane Jackson leaned over the dugout as Clay slipped into his blue Liberty Rebels letter jacket trimmed in gray.

Clay felt his knees grow slightly weak as he gazed at Diane's sea-green eyes in her heart-shaped face. The smooth skin across the bridge of her small nose was lightly freckled and her lips were full and pink-tinged and moist. "There's a fellow in the stands who might give you an argument about that," Clay smiled, glancing at the three men who were headed his way.

Several stragglers were following along after Williams, holding out papers and pens for autographs, but the majority of the Liberty fans had gotten theirs before the game.

Diane turned around to face the bleachers. "Why, it's just J.T. and some bald-headed man and—my goodness, it's Ted Williams! I recognize him from *Life* magazine."

As the crowd was dispersing, noisily reliving the most exciting plays of the game, several students and a few parents stopped by to congratulate Clay. He reddened slightly, uncomfortable with the adulation of his growing army of fans, not quite ready to accept his celebrity status.

Risemer leaned on the four-foot tall chain-link fence as Clay stepped out of the dugout. "Great game, son. I'm Benny Risemer, J.T.'s old buddy from Harvard."

15

"Y-yes sir," Clay stuttered, feeling awkward in the shadow of the game's greatest living player.

"Let me introduce you to Ted Williams," Risemer grinned. "You might have heard of him. He plays a little baseball from time to time."

Williams held out his hand. "How are you, Clay? I haven't seen pitching like that since I went down swinging at Bobby Feller's fastball."

"Thank, you sir." Clay shook Williams's hand, glancing at him, then over at Diane.

Clay introduced Diane while J.T. stood by beaming like a new daddy outside a maternity ward. He felt like handing out cigars.

"How'd you like to throw a few by me, Clay?" Williams asked in a level voice.

Clay merely smiled, kicking at the dirt with his cleats. When he looked up he saw that Williams was dead serious.

"C'mon, Mr. Williams," J.T. interrupted. "He just pitched nine innings."

"He'll have to pitch to twice as many batters as he did today if he makes it to the pro's."

"How do you feel, kid?" Risemer mopped his head, squinting in Clay's direction.

Clay glanced over at Diane, as if for assurance. "Fine. Let's do it."

*   *   *

Diane and J.T. went over to the bleachers, and Williams hopped the fence, stepping down into the dugout where he rummaged through a heavy canvas bag stacked with bats. Selecting one and grabbing an ancient catcher's mitt off the bench, he stepped back out.

"You expect me to catch this kid?" Risemer held his hands out pleadingly. "Look at these things. They're soft as Ebbits Field cotton candy."

Williams grinned mischievously, tossed the mitt to Risemer, and walked off toward home plate. Taking off his jacket along the way, he dropped it on top of the dugout.

"There's no disgrace in getting hit out of the park by Ted Williams," J.T. assured Clay nervously. "Just stay on your toes after you throw the pitch."

Glancing over at Diane again, Clay took off his jacket and headed out to the mound.

"The things I do for the Red Sox," Risemer grumbling under his breath wearily as he walked around to the gate following after Williams.

Most of the crowd had left, but a few, seeing what was happening on the field, took seats in the bleachers.

Clay thought he had been nervous with Ted Williams in the stands, but now he faced him in the batter's box. Sixty feet away, the man looked ten feet tall as he set his feet firmly in place and took a few practice swings.

"You want a few warmup pitches?" Williams called out, standing relaxed, resting the bat on his shoulder.

"I'm OK."

Williams took one more swing, then held his bat high, his hips shifting slightly as he dug in for the pitch.

Rubbing the ball briefly in both hands, Clay slipped his glove back on, went through his windup, and whipped his best fastball waist high down the center of the plate. The crack of the bat ended his brief dream of getting one past the Red Sox slugger.

With an effortless swing, Williams had connected dead center, sending the ball sailing over the center-field wall.

Clay watched the ball climb higher and higher against the blue curve of the sky. It had just begun to drop when it disappeared beyond a stand of tall pines.

Picking up the rosin bag, Clay fidgeted with it for a few seconds. He threw the next ball three feet over Risemer's outstretched mitt.

A few chuckles ran through the crowd.

"Let's see you do any better," Diane said angrily to Keith Demerie, whose father, Senator Tyson Demerie had gotten him classified 4-F.

Demerie, a burly, blond twenty-year-old, home from his job as a page at the state capitol, smirked back at her. "Your boyfriend ain't ready for the big leagues *yet*."

Williams took the ball from Risemer and walked out to the mound with an encouraging smile on his face.

Clay glanced up at him, then began kicking the hard-packed dirt with his cleats.

Handing the ball to Clay, Williams shrugged. "Don't let it bother you. You're going to get heckled by the best when you make the majors."

"Yes sir." Clay squinted in the late sunlight, trying to smile, but he couldn't quite pull it off.

Williams thumped the bat on the pitching rubber. "Everybody has to deal with nerves. You just settle down, and I'll tell you a story about somebody who helped me in a tough situation when we're finished out here."

"Thanks, Mr. Williams." Clay felt a little better as he watched him walk away.

Stopping, Williams turned and squinted back at Clay. "You've got a good compact windup—except on the fastball. You stretch it out a little—not much, but enough that any sharp-eyed hitter can see it coming."

Clay thought about what he had just heard. Trying to picture his windups in his mind, he realized that Williams was right. He could almost feel the slight difference when he threw the fastball. *He'll be expecting a curve after what he did to my fastball.*

Williams now stood in the batter's box, swinging his bat smoothly across the plate.

As Clay prepared to throw, he deliberately used his ordinary windup, but his mind was intent on the fastball. He threw it as hard as he had ever thrown a ball in his life, catching the inside corner of the plate just above knee level.

Surprised, Williams tried to adjust his swing to the unexpected speed at the last moment, but his bat whiffed by slightly late and an inch above the ball. He grinned broadly at the lanky young pitcher, nodding his head in approval.

Applause broke out in the stands, punctuated by cheers from Diane and J.T.

Williams motioned for Clay to follow him back to the dugout. *Might as well let him finish on a good note. I've seen all I need to anyway.*

* * *

Clay caught up to Williams as he picked his jacket up from the roof of the dugout and slipped it back on. "Thanks for letting me get that one past you. But you didn't have to do that—no one would have blamed me for not getting a strike on you."

"I've never deliberately missed a ball in my life, son," Williams scowled. "You better learn this is serious business if you plan to stay with it."

Caught off guard by the abruptness of his response, Clay stammered, "I-I'm sorry, sir. I just thought . . ."

Williams replaced the scowl with a boyish grin, not at all unusual for his mercurial personality. "Forget it. It'll make a good story for the news hounds when we play together in our first World Series game."

Clay felt like he had when he had gotten his first bike that Christmas morning years ago; he remembered that J.T. had bought it for him. "You said you had a story for me?"

Giving him a thoughtful glance, Williams walked into the dugout. "Come on down. I like the smell in here—just like every other one I've ever been in. No matter where you go in the country, dugouts all smell the same."

Clay glanced over at the fence where J.T. and Diane waited with Risemer, then went inside, sitting next to Williams on the scarred bench. In the open space between them, *J.T.—1917* was carved into the rough oak.

Williams stuffed his bat back into the heavy bag at the end of the bench, gazing thoughtfully out toward home plate where the team manager, a pie-faced boy of fifteen was heading out to collect the bases. "You know, I was just as nervous as you before I played my final game last year."

Clay stared at him with a look of amazement. He thought of how confident Williams always looked at the plate, even in the tightest situations.

"Yes sir, I was awake half the night in that hotel room in Philadelphia. September 27, 1941. It was cold and rainy, and I thought the games might be canceled. It's a night I'll never forget."

"You played a doubleheader the next day against the Athletics," Clay volunteered.

"That's right. I had my .400 average." Williams opened and closed his left hand, the muscles in his forearms rippling like small cables beneath the skin. "Ready to go into the record books. They even told me I didn't have to play."

"You mean so you wouldn't take a chance on losing your .400? That must have been some decision to make."

"It was pure agony until a friend of mine laid it on the line for me."

Clay remained silent, feeling like he was being let in on a little bit of history from the man who had made it.

"Hugh Duffey hit .438 for the Sox in 1894. He was coaching me a little at the time."

"You know Hugh Duffey?" Clay thought he had been out of the game for years. "My grandpa used to talk about him when I was a little boy."

"Well, ol' Hugh didn't believe in coddling us young players— wouldn't allow any prima donnas to come close to him." Williams smiled. "He told me, 'Look, kid, go up there and take your cuts. If you miss, you just don't deserve it.'"

Clay thought it was good advice and decided to remember it for the future.

"And he was right," Williams continued. "I went on out there and took my cuts."

"And hit four for five in the first game, including your thirty-seventh home run."

"How about the second game?" Williams glanced about the dugout, taking pleasure in the cleat marks, carvings, and other leavings of the hundreds who had found their way here giving to and taking from the game.

"Two for three," Clay replied quickly, "and you told the reporters that you didn't want anyone to say you 'walked in through the back door.'"

"I did say that, didn't I?" Williams grinned and stood up. "Maybe that's good advice too—like Duffey gave me. Don't ever go down with your bat on your shoulder, kid."

"Are you going in the service, Mr. Williams?" Clay wasn't sure if he should ask, but it seemed the natural thing to do.

"Sure. Isn't everybody?"

"I am," Clay agreed. "Just haven't decided which branch I'm going to join yet."

"They're making noises like they want me to go in Special Services," Williams said with a frown. "Fighter pilot—that sounds much better, don't you think?"

"Yes sir," Clay grinned. "Special Services would be kinda like getting in through the back door wouldn't it?"

Clapping Clay on the shoulder, Williams laughed, "It sure would, kid. You're gonna do just fine when you get to Boston. What do you say we both join up in the fall and have this thing over with by Christmas?"

"Fine with me."

Clay walked with Williams toward the fence where Diane waited for him with J.T. and Risemer. He had felt a sense of unreality at actually sitting in his home dugout talking with Ted Williams. His mind reeled with images of the majors—the thunderous roar of the huge crowds packed tightly into the stadium, the clipped grass and freshly striped and raked infield, his own name blaring over the loudspeakers when the lineup was announced, the headlines leaping at him from the morning newspapers, and that feeling that was like no other when the last batter went down swinging.

Farewells were said and the three men walked off together, J.T. listing slightly like a sloop in a gentle swell. Clay stood at the fence next to Diane watching them until they disappeared around the corner of the concession stand.

"Want to go to the picture show tonight?" Clay placed his arm across Diane's shoulders, pulling her gently to him.

"Sure." She lay her head against his shoulder. *For Whom the Bell Tolls* is playing. Gary Cooper and that Swedish girl, Ingrid Bergman, are in it."

"I read the book." Clay began walking toward the gym where a few stragglers from the team were filing into the locker room. He took his arm from Diane's shoulders and held her hand. "Hemingway's one of my favorites."

"Oh, you read everything," Diane said with mild admiration. "The story's kind of sad, isn't it?"

"Well, it takes place in Spain during their civil war." Clay thought of the war his own country was now fighting, which had started so suddenly and viciously that quiet Sunday morning last December with the bombing of Pearl Harbor. "I don't think there *are* any happy wars, Diane."

21

2

IT TOLLS FOR THEE

"Well, I guess you really liked that movie, didn't you?" Clay took the damp handkerchief Diane handed back to him as they walked out under the marquee of the Liberty Theater. "This one was a two-handkerchief tear-jerker. You finished yours off, and now mine's sopping wet, too."

Diane pushed Clay lightly on the shoulder. "Oh, hush! Women like to cry sometimes."

"I thought I'd cry myself for a while there," Clay remarked in mock sincerity.

"You did? When?"

"When I saw the price of the tickets." Clay smiled. "Twenty-five cents apiece. They must think this is some kind of Broadway opening night."

Ignoring his attempt at humor, Diane took Clay's arm with both hands as they walked among the thinning crowd of movie-goers and spoke to several of their friends. She wore a lavender sweater against the chill night air but still shivered slightly as an errant breeze swept past, sending leftover winter leaves scraping dryly along the sidewalk.

Without asking, Clay took off his letter jacket and draped it around her shoulders. Little acts of thoughtfulness like this always made him feel chivalrous, as though he were Sir Walter Scott laying his cloak across a puddle for the queen. "I don't think I've ever known you to wear warm enough clothes. You always manage to underdress."

Squeezing Clay's arm, Diane stood on tiptoe and whispered, "If you think I'm underdressed now, just wait till we get married." She turned her head away and blushed slightly even as she spoke the words.

23

Clay stared down at her, open-mouthed.

"Besides," Diane continued with mock arrogance in an attempt to cover up her embarrassment, "that's what I've got *you* for. To look out for me."

Clay felt his throat constricting at the thought of what Diane had said. Images of filmy nightgowns and silk stockings floated around at the back of his mind. He pushed them aside mentally and tried to control his voice, but it cracked slightly as he spoke. "Well, you sure *need* some looking out for all right."

Clay's reaction was not lost on Diane, and she felt an undefined sense of satisfaction at the effect she had on him. Suddenly, the last scene of the movie they had just seen came back to her. "Oh, Clay, I wish you didn't have to go in the army!"

"We've gotta whip the Japs before they start landing on the beaches in California," Clay responded, trying to sound like Brian Donlevy in *Wake Island*. "Everybody's joining up."

"Not everyone."

"Everybody that's healthy and not too old. It's every man's duty as an American." Clay felt suddenly as though his words had a hollow ring to them, as though he were playing a role that would eventually catch up to him.

"Keith Demerie isn't going. He's twenty years old and healthy as a horse."

Clay frowned down at Diane. "His daddy's a senator. Politicians always manage to pull off stunts like that for themselves or people they know."

"Daddy's got a lot of connections with the newspaper, Clay." Diane felt uneasy as she broached the subject but plunged ahead anyway. "I bet he could get you a job where you'd be excused from the draft."

They had come to the Liberty High campus. Pale light from the streetlamps fell across the grounds, casting murky shadows beneath the huge oaks. Clay led the way to one that stood close by, tilting the sidewalk with its roots, and sat on a stone bench beneath it. Diane sat next to him, afraid that she had offended him by what she had said about the job.

The schoolyard held a breathless silence as though resting from the activities and incessant noises of the day. With June approaching, the school bell would soon forfeit its clamorous authority, giving way to the long, indolent days and soft nights of summer.

Memories of all the years he had spent on these grounds flooded over Clay. He saw himself as a first grader, carrying his lunch in a brown paper sack; as a junior high student, when Bonner Ridgeway, the gravelly voiced coach first recognized his remarkable ability to throw a baseball. He remembered the first time he kissed Diane on this very bench when they both had to stay after school for passing notes in class.

It seemed to Clay that the night was wearing down to a kind of sadness. It weighed him down. He was experiencing the end of things before their rightful end; his childhood lay behind him, and he longed for and feared what lay ahead for him as a man. He could never admit to, nor even articulate, the emotions that raged through him at the most absurd times and for no apparent reason.

"Clay, I-I'm sorry if I said anything wrong," Diane said hesitantly. "I just can't bear the thought of you going off to war. What if . . ."

It took Clay a few seconds to realize who was talking to him. Diane's words seemed to be coming from a time years before. "Don't let it bother you. I know you're just worried about me—but I'd *never* do anything like that." He took her face in his hands, kissing her gently on the mouth. Her lips were parted and moist, and he was surprised at the eagerness of her response. He put his arms around her and lost himself in the warmth and wonder of this unexpected passion.

In a few seconds Diane pulled gently away. "There has to be something we can do."

Clay took her hand, squeezed it, and stared down the street at the series of streetlamps that led to the next block, disappearing from sight where the street curved around the base of a low hill.

"Are you OK, Clay?"

Laying his other hand on top of hers, he patted it gently. "I'm just fine."

"You're awfully quiet."

Clay took a deep breath. "I was just thinking about Lyle Oliver."

"I didn't know you were friends with him."

"I wasn't really. I knew him and Billy and Marcell Duke.

25

Marcell whipped the dog out of me in a fistfight in the locker room once." Clay gave Diane a half smile. "That's about as close as *we* ever came to being friends."

"Well, he was a lot older than you." Diane leaped to Clay's defense.

"Wouldn't have mattered. Marcell could knock a steam engine off the tracks with that right of his." Clay stared up at the star-filled sky. "It's funny to think of Lyle dead now and Billy and Marcell off in the Marine Corps. I think they're in boot camp at Parris Island. Seems like it was just last week we were all in school together right here."

Diane lay her head on Clay's shoulder, taking his hand in both of hers.

"I guess Lyle came to mind because he got killed at New Caledonia—wherever that is. Somewhere out in the Pacific is all I know about it. Billy Christmas told me that before he joined up." Clay felt himself tremble slightly and hoped that it was only in his mind—that Diane felt nothing. "A Jap mortar got him, and Billy said that his buddies carried him all the way back through the jungles to the ship—but he died anyway. He's buried out there on that island ten thousand miles away."

The distant lonesome whine of a heavy truck out on the highway gave voice to Clay's feelings.

"Billy told me about how Lyle's mother said that he got saved right before he joined the Marines. I didn't know what to say." Clay turned to Diane as though expecting a parable of explanation like he had heard about in the Bible.

"Saved from what?" She shrugged, trying to avoid any further discussion of the subject.

"Well, you and your family go to *church* every Sunday. What does it really mean?"

Diane fidgeted on the bench. "Daddy says it's expected of us—with him owning the newspaper and everything. He says religion is the 'opiate of the masses.'"

"What's *that* supposed to mean?" Clay responded with some irritation. "Makes about as much sense as saying, 'work is the curse of the drinking class.' I think it's gonna take more than a lot of fancy sayings to get us through this war."

"Let's not talk about things like that anymore." Diane climbed into Clay's lap. "Why don't we just pretend that there's no old war at all?"

"Fine with me." Clay shook off the memories, brightening with the feel of Diane, warm and soft against him.

"I know!" Diane slid off his lap, pulling him up from the bench. "Let's go to Ollie's for a malt."

Clay was concerned about Diane's wanting to get him out of the draft by using her father's influence—knew that it hinted at some deeper trait in her—but in the fashion of youth, somber thoughts proved too heavy to carry for more than a few moments. "Now you're talking some sense. A chocolate malt can take care of a whole lot of worries."

* * *

"Look over there! Ben's back!" Clay entered the neon glare of Ollie's Drugstore with Diane, walking across the black-and-white tiled floor to the marble-topped counter. "Hey, Ben. How's Liberty's only Medal-of-Honor winner doing these days?"

Ben Logan, wearing his simple Navy dungarees and light blue shirt, stood at the far end of the marble-topped counter. Just under six feet tall, he was lean and hard with black hair, piercing gray eyes, and finely chiseled features. Even after two months, the attention his decoration attracted still made him uneasy. "Real good, Clay. How 'bout you? Hi, Diane."

Clay shook his hand, clapping him on the back. "Them big shots in Washington still got you traveling all around the country selling war bonds?"

"Yep. Sometimes I think it's worse than boot camp." Ben shifted the subject away from himself. "Speaking of big shots, I thought I saw Ted Williams sittin' in the stands out at the ball game today."

"You sure did!" Diane chimed in, taking Clay's hand. "He came down here to get Clay to sign a contract with the Boston Red Sox."

"I always figured you'd make it to the majors someday, Clay." Ben grinned at Diane. "Even when we were kids, he could throw a rock over the tops of the trees on the other side of the swimmin' hole."

"How's Rachel, Ben?" Diane saw the "good ol' boy" stories coming and tried to head them off. "I hardly ever see her around town anymore."

"She's workin' down at Hightower's in the office after she gets out of school. She's going to night school at the college this summer to take some business courses—thinks it'll help her get a promotion."

"Y'all getting married?" The hottest news in town was what was happening in the life of the man who had been to the White House to meet the president, and Diane wanted to be the first to hear any juicy news about Ben.

"Not unless Tojo and Hitler both surrender on the same day," Ben laughed. "I think we'll wait till the war's over."

"Here's the medicine for your mama, Ben." Ollie Caston walked behind the counter from the door that led to the pharmacy and storage areas. His scalp gleamed through the short brown crew cut, and his black bow tie provided a neat punctuation mark for his white shirt and apron. "Hope she gets to feeling better."

"Thanks, Mr. Caston," Ben replied, taking the white paper bag. "I'll tell her you were asking about her."

Turning to Clay and Diane, Caston spoke with obvious pride. "And what can I get for the next strikeout king of the American League? And his lovely lady, of course."

"Two chocolate malts, Mr. Caston," Diane answered for them, "and make them thick."

"You ever get one here that wasn't thick?" Caston grinned. "How 'bout you, Ben? It's not often I get two big celebrities in here at one time."

"No thanks. I better get on home."

"It's on the house," Ollie offered. "It's not often you get *anything* for free in this world."

"Aw, c'mon, Ben," Clay complained. "It might be another year or two before we see each other again."

Sensing that Clay needed to talk to him, Ben quickly relented. "OK. I never could resist one of Ollie's malts."

"Y'all go sit down. I'll bring 'em over to you in just a minute." Ollie began scooping ice cream from a cardboard tub in the freezer beneath the counter, flinging it with practiced efficiency into a tall silver cup.

Clay glanced at the five marble-topped tables at the front of the drugstore near the plate-glass window. They were all filled, mostly by sailors and soldiers whose girls appeared duly impressed by their uniforms. "There's a place." He pointed to the last booth in a row of three against the far wall.

"I know you boys want to talk about old times," Diane admitted. "I see Angela Spain over there. I think I'll go try to find out what's happening with her."

As Ben watched Diane walk toward the first booth, Angela noticed him and waved. She brushed her long dark-brown hair back from her face with an enticing gesture that seemed as natural and unaffected as if she had been sitting alone at her dressing table. Her violet eyes were shaded by incredibly long lashes, and they closed slightly as she smiled at him.

Ben remembered that cold, rainy night four years earlier when he had followed Angela down a dimly lit hallway with gleaming hardwood floors and oil paintings in heavy gilt frames on the walls. He saw again the small alcove overlooking the backyard of the mansion; felt the softness of the wine-colored velvet cushions on the window seat. As he followed Clay to their seats, he nodded to Angela, forcing the memory from his mind.

Sliding into the booth, Clay remarked knowingly, "I'd sure like to hear what Angela tells Diane. I bet it'd make a drunk sailor blush."

Ben ignored the remark, gazing at a skinny, pasty-faced private in army green who was dropping nickels into the jukebox. As he returned to his table, "Praise the Lord and Pass the Ammunition" blared from the speaker.

"It's no wonder you never see her with her husband." Clay, like most other young men in Liberty, was fascinated by Angela Spain. "She can't be more than twenty-two, and he's thirty years older than that if he's a day. Guess Morton's just too old to keep up with her."

"Maybe he works a lot, Clay," Ben said flatly, trying to put an end to the discussion of Angela Spain. "How're your folks getting along?"

"Same as always," Clay shrugged. "Mama hardly ever goes anywhere and Daddy works all the time. I think Hartley Lambert would lay down and die if he had to give his men a day off, except for Christmas and Thanksgiving. I hated working at that place on Saturdays before I got on at the *Herald*—never even had a chance for a break."

Ben nodded and glanced up at Caston who set their malts on the table and rushed off to wait on four Marines who had just taken seats at the counter. They were gawky, in their late teens, and fresh out of boot camp.

"Mm, that's good." Ben drank directly from the tall glass, leaving a brown mustache across his lip. "I used to dream about Ollie's malts when I was at sea."

Clay sipped his malt thoughtfully through the straw. "Ben, what's it like? Being in battle, I mean?"

Taking another long swallow of the malt, Ben leaned back in the booth. "Hard to explain. For me it happened so fast it's all still kind of a blur."

"Yeah, I hear that the waiting around part before the fight is the worst thing about it." Clay wanted to hear some tried-and-true plan from Ben that he could use to take the chill of fear out of his thoughts about the war.

"I don't know about that. When those Jap planes hit us, the first thing I remember is looking down the barrel of that 20 mm cannon." Ben could see the uncertainty in Clay's face and knew that he was experiencing what all young men did as they left their school years for the prospect of facing an enemy who seemed invincible, or at the very least vicious and without principle. "You going to join up?"

"Yeah. Everybody I know is—just about."

"Decided what branch yet?"

Clay shook his head and took a sip of his malt.

"Navy's all right if you don't mind looking at a whole lot of water every day."

Clay smiled at Ben. Pushing the glass aside, he leaned both elbows on the table. "Maybe the Marines. If Billy and Marcell can do it, so can I. What do you think about that?"

"If you wanna fight that's the place to be all right." Ben had heard rumors about the island-hopping campaigns that were being planned in the South Pacific and knew the Marines would be the first ones on the beaches. *No sense in worrying Clay. Men are going to get killed everywhere in this war. Look how many went down with the*

Arizona. *I was almost one of them.* "They probably have the best training in the world."

"Don't Sit under the Apple Tree" by the Andrew Sisters began to play from the jukebox. One of the Marines, a short, stocky man who looked older than his three friends, slid off his stool at the counter. He had black hair and a swarthy face. Walking over to a table, he asked the skinny private's chubby girlfriend to dance.

The private was on his feet and in the Marine's face before he could finish his invitation. "She ain't got no truck with Jarheads— and neither do I."

The stocky man smirked at the skinny army private—then without warning, swung his big fist at the boy's pale face. The boy seemed to vanish as the blow expended itself on air. A fraction of a second later, the Marine's eyes bulged with surprise and pain as the young private buried his fist almost up to the wrist in the heavy man's stomach.

Hearing the commotion, Ben slipped out of his booth and grabbed the soldier from behind before he could straighten the Marine up with a smash to the chin.

"Let me go! I'll kill him!" The boy struggled against Ben, his arms pinned to his sides.

"Turn him loose!" the big Marine gasped. "He hit me from behind!" Then he gazed up at Clay, who had stepped in front of him. At six foot three and 190 pounds, Clay got the man's attention. Noticing Clay's arms and shoulders, corded with muscle from helping his dad at the lumberyard and years of sports, he decided that this was not a one-man job. Glancing at his three buddies, he saw that Caston already had them under control.

"C'mon, boys," Ollie grinned, a Louisville Slugger balanced lightly in one hand. "We're all on the same side in this war. Sit back down and have some ice cream on the house."

With some grumbling, the two men returned to their separate seats, scowling at each other as they parted. Ben and Clay walked back to their booth.

"I like the way you handled that, Sailor," Angela spoke under her breath as Ben passed her booth.

Ben glanced at her, his face reddening slightly, but didn't respond.

Diane joined them as they sat back down. "Well you two sure earned your malts tonight."

"How's Angela? She have any good stories for you?" Clay's smile was almost a leer.

"No, she didn't," Diane shot back. "And if she did, I certainly wouldn't tell you."

"You must have talked about something."

"Angela always looks so sad. I thought she could use some company."

"She doesn't look sad to me, and she has a whole lot of company from what I hear."

"You just wouldn't understand, Clay. Men never do about these things," Diane explained as though she were talking to a first grader. "She did tell me she saw poor ol' J.T. stumbling down the street on her way over here."

Clay's eyes narrowed in concern. "Maybe I better go look for him, help him get home all right."

"Want me to come with you?" Ben asked. "I've got Daddy's truck outside."

"Nah. I'll probably find him quicker on foot." Clay stood up and gave Diane a hand out of the booth. "I know where he usually winds up when he gets a snootfull. He'll head back down memory lane."

Ben swallowed the last of his malt, grabbed his paper bag, and joined Clay and Diane. "Guess I better get this medicine on back to Mama. Nice seeing y'all."

"Would you mind taking Diane home? I'll ride with you and then you can drop me off at the school. Sometimes J.T. ends up down there."

"Sure thing," Ben nodded. "You really like ol' J.T. don't you, Clay?"

Clay's eyes looked at something in the past. "He spent a lot of time with me when I was growing up. Daddy only had Sundays off, and he was always give out then."

As they were leaving, the skinny private dropped another nickel in the jukebox and leaned back against it, staring at the swarthy man who still sat at the counter with his buddies. When "This Is the Army, Mr. Jones" began playing, he returned to his girlfriend, scowling fiercely at the Marines.

"You gotta give him credit," Clay laughed. "The little guy's got courage."

Ben's face clouded over. "I hope so. He's gonna need a lot of it where he's going."

* * *

Clay walked across the parking lot toward the football stadium, his shoes crunching in the loose gravel. As he climbed the wooden steps and walked along the rail that followed the sideline, he glanced about looking for J.T. The fragrance of night-blooming jasmine hung in the cool air. Anemic light from streetlamps and nearby houses transformed the structure into the perfect refuge for dark shadows and darker thoughts.

In the first two or three months after the attack on Pearl Harbor, the people of Liberty imposed a blackout on their town. Now, after four months of parades and posters and political speeches, it was still in effect but few adhered to it, believing their country invincible.

Watching strips of wispy black clouds float across a quarter-moon, Clay caught a slight movement out of the corner of his eye. J.T., cast into silhouette at the very top of the stadium, lifted his silver flask to his lips. Feeling the need to shake off the unease that had settled over him since his talk with Ben, Clay sprinted up the steps, taking them two at a time.

"Clay, my boy." J.T. attempted to get up, but immediately lost his balance and thumped back down on the wooden bench. "Pardon me if I don't rise for the occasion. I seemed to have dropped my equilibrium back in the gravel."

Clay didn't smile as he gazed at J.T.'s swollen face. He affected the insidious grin of a court jester, but in the pale light his rheumy eyes seemed suffused with an unfathomable melancholy. "Why do you do this to yourself, J.T.?"

Sipping again from the flask, J.T. held it aloft and spoke in Shakespearian intonation, "'Twas for love I flung myself on Dionysus' altar.'"

"What?"

"For true love, my boy—mine, not hers." J.T. stood shakily to his feet, railing at the thin blade of a moon:

> "How like a winter hath my absence been
> From thee, the pleasure of the fleeting year!

What freezings have I felt what dark days seen!
What old December's bareness everywhere!"

Clay took him by the shoulders, easing him back down to his seat. "You're not making a lick of sense. Why don't you let me take you on home?"

"Don't care for the vaunted Bard, eh?" J.T., his eyes shining with alcohol, turned toward Clay. "Well, let me put it in the idiom of this cultural desert I find myself in. It was a woman that drove me to drink—and I never did write and thank her."

Nodding his head, Clay murmured, "I heard those stories about you and Ellie—before she married Hartley Lambert. You were the star quarterback on his way to Harvard Law School and she was queen of everything at Liberty High."

J.T. leaned back against the railing, his face slack with defeat as he stared listlessly down onto the field. "Ellie was my whole life—and she couldn't even wait for me to finish school."

"Maybe breaking hearts runs in her family," Clay mused.

A puzzled frown crossed J.T.'s face.

"Her daughter," Clay explained. "Look what Debbie did to Ben Logan when they were in school together."

"I remember that."

"Well, it looks like Ben got over it fine," Clay continued. "You can too."

"Ben got some help."

"Help?"

"Spiritual help, my boy," J.T. muttered. "He got religion sometime after he went in the Navy."

"Why don't you try it then?"

"I don't know. Maybe I'm too old to change—too set in my ways."

"Let's get on home now." Clay stood up, shivering slightly. He had forgotten to get his jacket back from Diane again. "You'll catch pneumonia out here."

"Religion," J.T., his face turned toward the heavens, mumbled to himself as though he were alone in the empty stadium. "'For we wrestle not against flesh and blood, but against principalities, against powers, against the rulers of the darkness of this world, against spiritual wickedness in high places.' Maybe that war is worse than the one we're fighting with Germany and Japan—or maybe they're the same war."

"You sure do know a lot about the Bible for somebody that don't care about religion."

J.T. turned to Clay as if just noticing him for the first time. "I read all the great literature. I've had plenty of time for it since I've . . . neglected my law practice."

Clay took J.T.'s hand and pulled him to his feet. The two of them walked slowly down the steps: a young man who would soon rush headlong into battle—an older one who engaged the enemy each morning when he rose to face another day.

3

LILA

Gazing at the paintless frame building whose windows had mostly fallen victim to that deadly amalgam of boys and rocks, Lila Creel felt her spirits sink. *Maybe I should have stayed in Chicago. At least I could count on a paycheck from the* Tribune *every week. No! I wouldn't live through another one of those winters no matter what!*

Lila pushed a few strands of her gray-blond hair that had worked free of her French roll back from her high forehead. Her strong chin and slightly upturned nose sometimes gave a false impression of arrogance rather than the determination that was a truer portrayal of her nature. Her intelligent gray eyes gazed disdainfully at the former home of the *Journal* that she had purchased with her life savings and her husband's insurance money.

Goldenrod, dandelions, and assorted other weeds and flowers grew in rampant disorder about the long-neglected lawn of the building. Spilling in a purple cascade from a broken-down trellis, wisteria lent an air of springtime gaiety to one end of the small front porch.

The yard had one redeeming feature: a magnificent oak. Its branches spread over the roof, sheltered most of the front lawn, and extended almost to the other side of the narrow, quiet street. The morning sunlight softly patterned the ground beneath the tree with shadow and drifted like green-gold smoke in its crown.

As she reluctantly followed the sidewalk to the porch and summoned her courage to face whatever awaited her inside the building—hoping that the press was in better shape than the yard—Lila noticed a man shambling down the sidewalk. He was about six feet tall, slim, and wore an expensive brown sport coat with khakis and scuffed work shoes.

Looks like he's down on his luck. Maybe he could use a few dollars. "Excuse me, but would you like to do some yard work for me?"

J.T. stopped at the end of the walk, taking in Lila's trim figure in her cream-colored silk blouse and tailored gray slacks. He started to walk on but something in her no-nonsense, straightforward approach struck a chord somewhere deep inside him. "You don't waste words, do you?"

"Usually not."

"You're not from around here," J.T. continued, his appetite now whetted for some conversation. "I'd certainly remember you if you were."

Lila looked closer at J.T. as he walked down the sidewalk toward her. He was decades older than when she had gone to school with him, of course, but even with the week-old growth of brown and gray beard and the disheveled appearance, she recognized him. "J.T. Dickerson. You played quarterback for Liberty High!"

Stunned, J.T. stopped in his tracks, trying to remember where he had met this confident and seemingly guileless female. He had seldom met a woman who appeared so self-assured. "I'm afraid you have me at a disadvantage."

"We went to school together."

"Are you certain? I think I would remember someone as striking as you."

Lila raised her delicate-looking hand to her throat in a graceful motion, then put it quickly back down as though she had violated some kind of self-imposed rule. "No you wouldn't. I was a rather *unobtrusive* freshman, and you were a senior football star. That's like two people living on different planets."

J.T. tried to picture Lila as a fourteen-year-old but couldn't get the image in focus.

"My name was Lila Kronen. I'm planning to use my maiden name again now that I've come home."

J.T. remembered the family but not Lila. "Your daddy was a conductor on the railroad."

"Yes, he was," Lila smiled. "We moved to Chicago at the end of my freshman year when Daddy got a promotion. It's a bit different from the South."

"So I've heard."

Lila stepped up onto the porch, seeing in J.T.'s eyes that, even with her prompting, he remembered only her daddy. It was as though she were in the ninth grade again. She glanced around at the screen door hanging from one hinge and the leaves and scraps of paper collected against the wall. Turning back toward J.T. she made an obvious study of his rumpled appearance. "As I remember, you had been accepted by Harvard Law School."

"Yep." J.T. walked over to the porch and sat down, leaning back against a once-white column. "Course you don't want to be too hard on them. Even men who run revered institutions like Harvard occasionally succumb to human frailties. Not only did they admit me, they let me graduate."

"Oh, I didn't mean . . ." Lila began.

"Yes, you most assuredly did," J.T. interrupted her. Then he gave her a warm smile. "And I probably deserve it—for some reason or other."

Lila felt the color rise in her face. "No, you don't."

"You mean I didn't offend you somehow when we were in school together? I didn't miss many." J.T. watched her walk the few steps to a porch swing, test it for stability, and sit carefully down. "I was pretty full of myself back then."

"No, you didn't even know I was alive," Lila confessed, swinging gently back and forth. "I guess maybe that's it. You had everything—including the prettiest girl in school. 'And he glittered when he walked.'"

J.T. thought of the ending of the poem by E. A. Robinson that Lila was quoting from. "Let's hope I don't end up like Richard Cory did."

Lila stared into J.T.'s deep brown eyes, sensing something that caused her to look quickly away. "Oh, you won't! Don't even think such a thing!"

Seeing that he had made her uncomfortable, J.T. changed the subject. "You buy this place?"

"Yes. I'm beginning to think I made a mistake." Lila frowned at the wrecked screen door.

"Calvin sell it to you?" J.T. asked, referring to the mayor who also owned Sinclair Real Estate.

"Why, yes. How did *you* know that?"

"Ol' Calvin has a tendency to—*romanticize* the properties he has listed on occasion." J.T. grinned, looking at the old building. "This place is solid though. Made out of heart-pine timbers a termite would break his teeth on."

Lila gave J.T. a half smile, still trying to figure out whether she liked him or not. "I'm sorry I asked you to do the yard work. I didn't know you were a lawyer."

"Forget it." J.T. shrugged. "I'll be over here first thing in the morning."

"Oh, no, I couldn't let you do that!" Lila waved her hand as if dismissing the suggestion that a Harvard graduate should do yard work. "Forget I asked."

"It was a valid offer and I accept." J.T. grinned. "Besides, I could use the exercise—and the money."

Lila found J.T.'s willingness to do manual labor a refreshing change from the attitudes of the professional men she had known in Chicago. "Well—all right."

"You really going try to publish the *Journal* again?"

"That's what I had in mind. I hope the machinery inside is in good shape."

"You have any experience in the newspaper business?" J.T. gave her a skeptical glance.

"Twenty years at the *Tribune*."

"That oughta help some." J.T. nodded as he glanced at a squirrel scampering up the massive trunk of the oak. With his face turned away from Lila he asked, "Is your husband in the newspaper business, too?"

"No." Lila's voice took on a somber tone. "Howard was an invalid for the last fifteen years of his life. He died on Christmas Eve."

"I'm sorry." J.T. got up and walked across the porch, pushing the screen door carefully aside and testing the brass knob on the heavy oak door. It swung smoothly inward. "Let's see if it looks any better inside."

Lila eased out of the swing and followed J.T. into the front reception area. The counter was cluttered with old folders, and a five-year-old Hightower's Department Store calender hung on one wall. Offices on either side of the reception area were furnished with heavy antique desks and wooden swivel chairs. Dust coated everything, including the hardwood floors that nonetheless still retained some of their gloss.

"I've seen worse," J.T. said matter-of-factly, walking into the long, cement-floored room in back. Banks of windows ran along the high ceiling on both side walls all the way to the back of the building where an overhead door led out onto a loading dock. A few rolls of newsprint lay scattered about. Like the front offices, dust lay like a blanket on everything. "I'm no expert, but it looks like the press is in pretty good shape."

Lila walked about, inspecting everything carefully. "It's much better than I had expected after seeing the outside. Looks like cleaning is all it really needs."

J.T. continued on to the back, walking out onto the loading dock. Flipping a wooden spool on end with his foot, he sat down. "I'd like to see the *Journal* coming off the presses again."

Walking over to the edge of the loading dock, Lila gazed at the weeds growing along its base and out of the cracks in the concrete ramp below. "You have an interest in the publishing business, Mr. Dickerson?"

"J.T.—please! You make me sound so respectable." He stood up and walked over to where she stood. "I have an interest in seeing that Dobe Jackson doesn't have so much influence over public opinion in this town."

"He owns the *Liberty Herald*, doesn't he?"

"That's right. And Dobe could stand a little competition. Might make him a little less grandiose in those pontifications he calls editorials."

With J.T. so close to her, Lila could smell the alcohol that seemed to be seeping out of his pores. "Sounds like you don't particularly care for him."

J.T. merely grunted. "You got a typesetter?"

"The best. Typesetter and layout man. He's got real printer's ink flowing in his veins and all the other old clichés of the newspaper game." Lila's expression turned inward as she thought of her longtime friend. "His name's Henry Steinberg, and he's retired from the *Tribune*."

"Well, you've got a good start." Without further discussion, J.T. walked down the concrete steps at the side of the loading ramp and headed down the driveway at the side of the building.

Caught by surprise at the abruptness of his departure, Lila stammered, "B-but, I thought . . ."

"See you tomorrow." J.T. waved over his shoulder.

* * *

Henry Steinberg waved to Lila as she entered the restaurant of the Liberty Hotel. He stood to his full five-foot-six inches, two inches taller than Lila, as she weaved her way through the early morning crowd over to his table next to the window.

Henry's neat white mustache twitched beneath his stub of a nose when he became nervous, and he was very nervous now on this, his first trip to the deep South. His eyebrows, bristly imitations of the mustache, perched like fuzzy caterpillars above the deep-set dark eyes. Parted in the middle, his thin white hair lay close to his head. He smelled mildly of witch hazel.

"Morning, Henry." Lila smiled, taking the chair he had pulled out for her.

"Good morning," Henry replied, slipping quickly back into his seat.

"My, you certainly look dapper this morning," Lila observed, noticing his neat dark suit and bow tie. "But then you always were a stylish dresser."

Even at the age of sixty-seven, or perhaps *especially* at the age of sixty-seven, Henry, like most men, was susceptible to flattery. It seemed to give him a sense of confidence. "Thank you, Lila. You just made an old man's day."

Lila glanced over her shoulder, motioning to the waitress. "You may be the youngest man I know, Henry."

After the waitress brought coffee and they had ordered breakfast, Lila spooned sugar into her cup, adding a dollop of thick, pale yellow cream. "Umm, that's so good! I'd forgotten what real coffee tastes like."

"It's strong, but it does have a certain body to it, doesn't it?" Henry mused, preferring to sip his black, having developed the habit at work when the pressures of the job made it more efficient to grab a cup and run.

"What time did your train get in?" Lila felt comfortable having an old friend like Henry in town as most of the people she had known—the ones who were still alive—were now little more than strangers to her.

"Midnight or thereabouts. I walked here from the station. Got to see some of the town." He glanced around the room. "It's a nice place."

Lila breathed in the heady and distinct smells of Southern breakfasts being served at the tables near them. "Then you won't mind living here for a month or two until we see how things are going to work out at the paper?"

"Not at all."

The waitress returned, setting the steaming plates of food in front of them. She had short blond hair. "I know ya'll ain't from around here. I hope you like the food."

"It looks wonderful," Lila assured her.

After refilling their coffee cups, she waddled off toward the double swinging doors that led into the kitchen.

"What's this?" Henry pointed to a pile of grits that dripped with butter.

"Grits," Lila informed him, slicing off a portion of patty sausage and chewing it with relish. "I told you about them. Go ahead—you might be surprised by how good they are."

"I don't think I want to rush headlong into this Southern culture."

"Where's your spirit of adventure, Henry?"

"Now that looks respectable," Henry ventured, pointing to the sausage Lila was eating. He cut off a piece of his own and held it in front of his mouth with his fork. "Is it good?"

"It is if you like possum."

Henry dropped his fork as if it had suddenly grown hot and it clattered to the plate. "Oh, Lord! Possum?"

Lila tried to keep a straight face but couldn't hold it. "No, Henry, it's just plain old pork sausage like we have in Chicago," she laughed. "Maybe a little spicier."

As they ate, Lila noticed that Henry devoured the sausage, eggs, and the homemade biscuits with their brown, flaky crusts and soft chewy insides. But he never let his fork touch the grits. When he had finished, all that remained was a white congealed mound standing like a culinary wallflower at the edge of his plate.

"What's your new business look like?" Henry asked over a fresh cup of coffee.

Lila glanced at Henry, then stared out the window. The street lay in heavy shade from the ancient elms that lined it. People walked at their leisure along the sidewalks on their way to work or to shop or simply to be out on such a bright May morning. She noticed the decidedly older and female composition of the people, as most of the able-bodied men were at the war or traveling to it or training for it. "I think you'd better make that determination for yourself."

"It's not that bad, is it?"

"The press looks OK, but the building isn't what you'd call palatial."

"Utility is what I'm used to anyway." Henry placed the tips of his forefingers together and rested his chin on them. "Give me a decent press and a place to work, and I'll be happy. After two years, I can't wait to get my hands stained again."

Lila felt comforted by Henry's solid, reassuring dedication to work and his competence in his trade. "You'll be the heart of the business, old friend."

"And you'll be the spirit—and the soul." Henry grinned. "Let's go see it."

*   *   *

J.T. had taken his shirt off and the waistband of his khakis was stained dark with sweat. Over the years, during his ever-decreasing periods of sobriety, he had always gone back to an exercise routine—a holdover from his years of participating in sports in high school and college. Now, although out of shape, his muscles still rippled smoothly under his white skin as he swung the swingblade, sending tall weeds flying before it in a storm of green. He had finished most of the front yard by the time Lila drove up in her green Plymouth coupe with Henry.

After Lila had introduced them, she surveyed J.T.'s work. "What time did you start?"

"Sunup." J.T. leaned on the swingblade. "This is the most fun I've had since my last root canal."

"I'll bet you didn't learn how to do this at Harvard," Lila smiled, surveying his work.

"Nope. I never had a course that made this much sense up there."

"I'm going to show Henry around," Lila said, motioning for

him to follow her. "I think you'd better take a break before you get heatstroke."

J.T. stretched the muscles of his arms and back. "Not just yet. It's become a personal grudge match between me and the weeds—who'll give in first."

Lila smiled and dodged a flying swatch of weeds as J.T. went back to work.

Inside the building, Henry walked briefly about the front offices before going into the back area where the real work was to take place. He walked slowly around the printing press, poking into narrow openings with a trained finger, bending, kneeling, stooping, and covering every inch of it with his practiced eye. Then he completed another circuit, stopping occasionally to make adjustments with an assortment of spotlessly maintained tools he took from a small, brown leather satchel.

"What do you think, Henry?" Lila had stood by silently, knowing that Henry took to his work with a tireless devotion and surgical precision.

Henry put the final instrument back in his case, closing it with a flick of his wrist. "I think this is going to be a lot of fun—that's what I think."

Lila breathed a sigh of relief. "You think the machine's all right then?"

"It's a beauty," Henry beamed, turning back to look lovingly at the dusty press.

"Thank the Lord. I was so afraid there might be something major wrong with it." Lila gazed at the dust particles dancing slowly in the sunlight that streamed in through the high windows. "My budget wouldn't handle expensive repairs."

"Where do we start?"

"I guess we help J.T. outside." Lila began walking toward the front with Henry close by her side. "Then these offices," she said, stepping into the reception area. "And finally we'll tackle this back area. It'll take a while I'm afraid."

Henry nodded toward the window. Outside, J.T. was still flailing away at his green enemy. "How does he fit into the scheme of things?"

Lila leaned against the counter. "I haven't quite figured it out myself yet."

"Do you know him, or is he just someone you flagged down on the street to help?"

Lila thought about the question for a moment. "Both I guess." Then she explained who J.T. was.

"Why would a Harvard lawyer want to work like a hired hand?"

"I have an idea his practice isn't exactly booming," Lila explained "His breath smelled like a miniature distillery when he stopped by yesterday."

Henry frowned at her. "I don't care if he is a part of your glorious Southern past, Lila, we don't need to involve some winehead in this little enterprise."

"I think there's a gentleman somewhere beneath all that crusty exterior, Henry," Lila mused, staring out the window. "Besides I'm only hiring someone to help us get this place in shape—not marrying him you know."

* * *

Lila sat at the same table in the Liberty Hotel's restaurant where she had had breakfast that morning, only now J.T. sat across from her instead of Henry. It was eight-thirty, late for a weeknight in Liberty, and only a few customers remained. Two waitresses plodded among the tables after their long day's work, cleaning up the last few dishes. Another stood near the cash register; a cigarette dangled from the side of her mouth as she added up her receipts for the day.

J.T. took a final bite of banana pudding, leaned back with a long sigh, and folded his hands across his lean stomach. "Boy, that was good. I'd forgotten what an appetite a hard day's work can give a man."

"You certainly put in a day's work all right," Lila agreed, sipping her coffee.

They had both gone home, J.T. to his office and Lila to the hotel, and cleaned up before meeting in the restaurant. Lila wore a simple pale blue dress with tiny yellow-and-white flowers on it. J.T. had put on his last clean white shirt, which he had picked up at the cleaners the month before, and had pressed most of the wrinkles out of his cleanest khakis.

"I feel better than I have in a long time—bone tired but good." J.T. gazed into Lila's eyes, causing her to glance out the window. "Reminds me of when I used to saw logs with Earl Logan during the summers. His daddy was a logger and a pulpwood man, and we'd work for him to make a little spending money."

"I saw a picture of a sailor named Logan on the cover of *Life* magazine. He stuck in my mind because he was from here." Lila looked back at J.T., noticing the flush of sunburn on his face. "The president decorated him with the Medal of Honor."

"That's Earl's boy. He sure turned out better than anybody in this town thought he would—including his daddy."

"I'm finding the old hometown is more interesting than I'd remembered." Lila reflected briefly on the past. Boring was the word that came to mind. As she let her gaze wander around the restaurant, she noticed a young dark-haired girl seated at a table in the far corner with a sailor who sported a thin mustache and a boyish smile on his tanned face. "For instance, that looks like an interesting pair over there. I'll bet they're high school sweethearts out for a final evening before he goes overseas."

J.T. glanced over his shoulder. "You'd lose."

Lila gave him a quizzical look.

"I never saw the boy before, so chances are he's just passing through."

"And the girl?"

"That's Angela Spain, she's only twenty-two and she's married to Morton Spain. He's a lawyer who's twice her age—at least."

"Well, she certainly is lovely."

"That's about the only thing that girl has going for her." J.T.'s voice carried a weariness in it that went deeper than just a hard day's work.

Lila had become intrigued by the prospect of finding out more about Angela, and her expression suggested it to J.T.

"She grew up in a shack outside of town—poor as Job's turkey." J.T. took a final swallow of his coffee. "Her daddy ran off and left her mama and her and her month-old brother. The boy died of pneumonia that winter."

Lila's eyes glistened with interest.

"Like I said, looks was all Angela had. When Morton's wife

was killed in a car wreck, she managed to—get his attention you might say, and in six months they got married. She couldn't have been more'n seventeen at the time."

"He must know this kind of thing is going on in a town this small." Lila glanced over her shoulder at Angela who was holding the sailor's hand across the table.

J.T. stared out the window at an old Negro man, shambling down the street in threadbare overalls and brogans. "I think he knew it would happen when he married her. But there ain't a whole lot of men who use good sense when it comes to picking the right woman."

"It's kind of sad for both of them, isn't it?" Lila stared at Angela, feeling her own loss and all the years that she now struggled to believe weren't wasted.

"Yeah, well I guess most of our wounds are self-inflicted—including Angela's."

Lila felt a twinge of anger stirring in her breast. "That's a rather callous attitude, isn't it?"

Noticing the slight flush in Lila's cheeks, J.T. realized that his remark probably came from his not having had a drink all day. He thought of the half-full bottle in the drawer of his desk. "Well, sometimes it's more callous in the long run when people *ignore* the truth."

"I'm not talking about *ignoring* anything. I'm talking about having a little understanding for human frailty." Lila felt the evening drifting into ruin and decided to stave it off. "I think I'll go on up to bed. It's been a long day."

"Yes, it has." J.T. grabbed the check from the table, stood up, and headed across the almost deserted restaurant toward the cashier, leaving Lila still seated.

"Are you coming back tomorrow?" She called to him, turning around in her chair.

J.T. stopped and gazed back at her. "I don't know yet. Expect me when you see me."

Part 2

THE ROSE-COLORED AFTERGLOW

4

ANGELA

*T*he narrow, rutted gravel road ran across the rolling pine barrens to the west, leading toward Liberty. Where it dropped out of sight behind a low ridge, the red sun burned against a hard winter sky.

At the bottom of the long, slow climb of the road, woods began with an overgrown path that led beneath huge oaks and beeches to a clapboard shack. Kudzu had climbed halfway up its walls and had reached long tentacles through the bare windows and along the rotted front porch. Now, in mid-December, the leafless vines looked like the gray skeleton of some amorphous and primordial beast that had been locked in a death grip with the ramshackle building.

In the rose-colored afterglow, Angela Spain stood next to her black LaSalle, parked on the bare ground at the side of the road where the path began. Her face held a pale and remote beauty, the porcelain sheen of her skin a marked contrast to her deep violet eyes and long dark lashes. She pulled her mink coat closer about her as the wind rustled through a few dry leaves that clung stubbornly to the oak limbs above the road.

Angela was eighteen, had been married six months and, one hour and twenty-five minutes earlier, had been unfaithful to her husband for the first time. Afterward, she had felt inexorably drawn back to this place where she was born and had lived the first seventeen years of her life.

She could almost see herself as a little girl in her printed floursack dress trudging up from the little stream that ran behind the house. Her syrup bucket full of water spilled over its shiny sides as she stumbled over a root, falling headlong onto the hard-packed dirt of the path. Dusting herself off, she set her jaw, picked up the bucket, and headed back through the dusty gloom of the late after-noon woods.

Angela walked slowly toward the little building as the twilight settled like gray-green smoke through the trees. She remembered the day her father had left them. She had been about eleven. Her mother had stood on the front porch holding Angela's infant brother as her father carried his cardboard suitcase out to the road, squinted into the rising sun to his left, and disappeared behind the trees and underbrush as he headed west down the gravel road.

At fifteen Angela had blossomed, and at seventeen her mother had managed to have her meet Morton Spain, who had been a wid-ower for less than a year. A few months later, they were married amid howls of protest from Spain's son, Taylor, who was not much younger than Angela.

Angela's mother had dreamed of living in the apartment above the garage behind Spain's mansion and got her wish. But she was to enjoy the fruits of her less-than-honorable labor only until the following Thanksgiving when, like her infant son, she too died of pneumonia.

Sitting down on the ruined porch, Angela took a half-pint bottle of scotch from inside her coat, and, unscrewing the top, took another quick swallow. Frowning with distaste, she took two more swallows and put the bottle away. A placid look came over her face as the alcohol burned her throat and stomach, flowing warmly through her veins until the sharp-edged uncertainties of her life seemed dulled and blunted and bearable.

*　*　*

"Where in the world have you been all day?" Morton Spain, clad in soft leather slippers and a burgundy bathrobe, stood at the top of the concrete steps that led from his portico to the back door of his huge home on Peachtree Boulevard. His red-rimmed eyes, the pouches beneath them purple tinted and permanent, glared at Angela through the window of her LaSalle as he continued his ti-rade. "You're hardly ever here anymore when I get home from work!"

Angela took a deep breath, slid out of the car, and walked around it toward her husband. Leaning against one of the columns that was a miniature of the huge white ones on the front of the house, she took off one of her high-heeled shoes and rapped it against the base to loosen a bit of mud stuck to the sole.

Spain ran his hand nervously over the few strands of graying black hair that covered his shiny head. "Well, aren't you going to give an account of yourself?"

Angela glanced up at her husband. The wrinkled skin under his neck hung loosely above his paunch, dwarfing his thin shoulders and chest. She thought briefly of the man she had been with only a few hours earlier and of how she had sat at the window after he had gone, watching a convoy of olive drab army trucks roar by on the highway in a seemingly endless line as they headed east. "I went out to the old shack."

"You mean that place where you grew up?" Spain had found Angela's behavior for the past month increasingly more difficult to deal with. He was used to conformity and dependability, qualities that she seemed to abhor with a vengeance. "Whatever for?"

"I don't really know." Angela shrugged, slipping her shoe back on.

Spain watched her climb the steps toward him. The flickering light from the wrought-iron gas lamps danced in the sheen of her long dark hair, and he felt his chest constrict as he tried to control his anger. "I'm worried about you, darling. Are you feeling well?"

"I'm all right."

Following her into the house, through the rear foyer, and into the kitchen, Spain watched her walk to the stove and pour herself a cup of strong black coffee. "I'd like one myself if you don't mind, sweetheart."

"Fine with me." Angela sat down, still wrapped in her mink coat, at the formica-topped table and spooned sugar into the steaming coffee.

Spain poured himself a cup of coffee and sat down with her. "Angela, I know your mother's death has been a terrible blow to you, but you're going to have to get yourself together. We can have a good life here."

Angela gazed into her husband's sad, dark eyes, feeling little more than pity for him—and disgust with herself. He had done everything he could to make her happy, refusing to accept what everyone else in town knew—that she had married him at her mother's insistence to escape the short slide into the poorhouse that was their obvious fate. "I know we can, Morton," Angela lied, taking his hand across the table.

"That's my girl." Spain's face brightened. "Why don't we fly to Atlanta this weekend: take in a show, eat at some disgustingly expensive restaurants? You know how you love the shopping there."

Forcing herself to smile, Angela nodded. "You're a good husband, Morton. I don't deserve you."

"Don't say such silly things, darling. After the terrible time you had growing up, you deserve *some* happiness in this life, and I'm just the one who can give it to you." Spain felt like a fifteen-year-old again just being in Angela's presence.

"But what can I give you in return?" Angela held his gaze over the rim of her coffee cup.

"Well, why don't you go and have your bath and slip into something comfortable, and I'll bring some chilled champagne and iced shrimp to your room." Spain's expression was that of a four-year-old waking on Christmas morning.

Angela sighed deeply. "I'm really bushed tonight, Morton. Maybe tomorrow."

Spain's face dropped, but he quickly regained control. "You do look a little weary."

Angela got up and kissed him on the top of his head. "Good night," she crooned as she left the kitchen.

"Good night, sweetheart," Spain muttered wearily. "See you in the morning."

Angela's heels clicked on the gleaming hardwood floors of the dimly lit hallway. Oil paintings in heavy gilt frames hung along the walls. The faces of generations of Spain's family seemed to glare down on Angela as though she had no right to enjoy the comfort and muted splendor of the house.

As the first note sounded from the piano, Angela stopped, listening to the music that drifted through the quiet and scented air. "Stardust"—her favorite. Removing her shoes, she quietly entered the drawing room. The heavy jade green curtains had been closed against the streetlights, and a brass floor lamp cast an amber glow about the room.

Taylor Spain sat at the piano, his eyes closed as his slim fingers moved skillfully across the dull-yellow ivory keys. He had dark hair and fine features and would have been handsome except for the acne that marked his face like a cruel joke.

Angela dropped her coat on the arm of a divan and sat down, curling her legs beneath her as she leaned back, savoring the lovely, delicate, bittersweet melody of the song.

The song finished, Taylor opened his eyes and glared at Angela. "What do you want?"

Angela smoothed her black wool skirt across her knees. "I want us to be friends."

Taylor merely grunted and began flipping through the sheet music on the piano.

"I mean it, Taylor." Angela's voice was soft and clear, inviting as a soft bed at the end of a long day.

"I like to pick my own friends," Taylor mumbled, glancing through the music.

Angela stood up and moved slowly across the room, her stockinged feet whispering on the plush wool rug.

Taylor forced himself not to look at her, and willed his mind free of fantasies.

Stopping at the edge of the baby grand, Angela leaned on it with one elbow. "Taylor . . . my only brother died when he was just a baby. I hoped we could be . . . kind of like a brother and sister, a real family."

"You married my father. Why don't you try being a *wife* to him for a change?"

"I respect your father very much." Angela felt the words sticking in her throat. "He's a kind and gentle man, and he takes good care of me."

"You haven't answered my question."

Angela put her hand to her mouth, chewing at the flaking polish of a fingernail.

"You've made our family a laughingstock. I'm ashamed to be a part of this family." Taylor lifted a piece of sheet music out of the stack and placed it in front of him.

Angela flinched as he played the first few bars of the song with a new energy. Without speaking, she turned and left the room. Walking down the long hall toward her bedroom, she felt the notes of "The Lady Is a Tramp" strike her back like thrown stones. The heavy bedroom door gave her a sense of comfort as she closed it and locked it.

Muted light from a streetlamp shone through the long diaphanous curtains, giving the darkened room an underwater quality. Angela lay across her bed, staring at the ceiling. She tried to put all thoughts from her mind, but memories clicked on and off like moths flickering in and out of a beam of light.

After a long while, Angela rose wearily from the bed and went into her bathroom to soak in a tub of hot water. After slipping into her nightgown, she turned down her covers and stood at the side of her bed. With effort, she flicked on the bedside lamp and opened the drawer of her nightstand. She dug to the bottom of the drawer and retrieved a brown paper bag, flattened and worn.

Angela lay back on the pillow, stared at the bag for a few seconds then opened it and took out a faded black-and-white print. As was her nightly habit, she smoothed its crinkled surface and held it under the amber glow of the lamp. It was the only picture she had left of her father. He stood in front of the little shack next to her mother, pregnant with her second child. Smiling wistfully, she held onto her husband's arm as she leaned against him.

As always, Angela was drawn to her father's eyes as they stared at something outside the frame of the picture. She had wondered for years what he had been looking at in that long-ago and lost moment of time when the camera's shutter snapped. Then she let her eyes wander behind her mother and father to the porch where she saw herself as a thin, almost hollow-eyed ten-year-old, staring at her father as though he were more apparition than flesh and blood.

After putting the photograph away, Angela turned out the lamp and lay staring at the long curtains. They seemed to be collecting the weak light from outside, trying to store it inside their wispy translucent folds. She tried to think of where her life was taking her, but the future seemed remote as a fable.

* * *

"We'll have those little yellow savages whipped in six month's time with men like Ben Logan fighting for this country." Morton Spain aligned himself with the heroes, although he knew full well there would be no fighting for *him* in this war just as there hadn't been in the last.

Angela walked along the station platform next to her husband, observing the huge turnout for Ben's homecoming. Red, white, and blue bunting had been strung from all the buildings, poles, and trees in the vicinity of the railroad station. Streamers of crepe paper and American flags fluttered in the breeze. "Welcome Home Ben" signs abounded in the hands of the people and were tacked to virtually any stationary and upright object. "This is quite a turnout for someone who was run out of town."

Spain cleared his throat. "Well, he—ah, wasn't actually run out of town as I recall."

"Oh, c'mon, Morton," Angela objected, knowing that her husband had always refused to discuss the subject. "Ben beat up Keith Demerie in Ollie's Drugstore—a public place. You think anyone believes the good Senator would let that happen to his son without getting his pound of flesh—one way or another?"

Spain gazed down the platform where the high school band was assembling in preparation for their customary off-key rendition of "Stars and Stripes Forever."

"Here we are, like everyone else in town, waiting to welcome home Liberty's biggest hero as if we had all been right there with him on the deck of the *Arizona* shooting down those Jap planes." In spite of their surroundings, Angela felt compelled to press the issue of what had happened to Ben Logan. "But where were we when he needed somebody to stand up for him?"

"Whatever happened, it turned out for the best, Angela," Spain snorted. "Let it be, will you?"

"Someone told me you sat in as ad hoc judge the day Ben came to court." Angela let her words sink in as she watched the back of her husband's neck redden slightly.

Spain pointed down the tracks. "Here it comes, right on time," he said, as if dismissing Angela's words. "Too bad everyone's not as reliable as that train."

"You forced him somehow to join the Navy just to get him out of town, didn't you, Morton?"

Glancing down at his wife, Spain set his jaw when he spoke. "It was for the boy's own good. He was just throwing his life away here selling moonshine."

"Well goodness knows we can't have that kind of thing going on, can we?" Angela knew that Moon Mullins' still had been an institution in the town for years.

"We can't have him committing assault and battery." The day had started well, but Spain felt it beginning to slip away. "Something had to be done."

"It was a fight between two seventeen-year-old boys, Morton—and Keith outweighed him by forty pounds." Angela felt herself deriving a perverse pleasure out of this exchange with her husband. "If you locked up people every time we had a fistfight in this town, the streets would be deserted."

Spain felt anger burning deep in his chest. Glancing around at the crowd, he struggled to restrain himself. "I think it's time we dropped this subject."

Angela remembered how suspicious her husband had been years before when Ben had made deliveries from Ollie's Drugstore to their home; she had seen the yellow gleam of jealousy in his eyes. "No reason to get angry, Morton. After all, he was only a boy. But he certainly changed after he went into the Navy."

Spain's dark eyes burned with the onset of rage as he turned them on Angela. "I won't have you speaking like this in public, Angela."

Taking his arm, Angela reached up and straightened his tie. "Why, Morton, whatever has upset you so? You know you don't have a thing to worry about with me."

Angela walked along next to her husband, sensing that he was cooling down as she spoke brightly about the events of the day. Her attitude had changed to that of the loving, devoted wife. She didn't understand this need to torment her husband but knew that it came from some dark place inside her—a place she was afraid to shine the light on. It was as though she were punishing him for sins someone else had committed.

"Hello, Mayor," Spain greeted the little mayor with a slightly amused smile as he always did. "Everything going to suit you with the homecoming?" Bored, Angela wandered away while they talked.

Calvin Sinclair wriggled his tiny black mustache as he spoke. He looked like a slightly overweight Charlie Chaplin, reminding people of the Little Tramp character in silent films. "If I can find room for about a thousand people on that twenty-by-twenty foot speaker's platform, everything will be just fine. Everybody in town claims to be Ben's close kin or his lifelong buddy."

"Well I, for one, am content to stand down here among the masses," Spain replied magnanimously.

Sinclair squinted up at Spain. "I should hope so, Morton. I imagine you're the *last* person Ben Logan wants to see when he gets back home."

"I was only seeing that justice was done," Spain snapped at Sinclair. "You didn't know Logan was alive till you saw his picture on the cover of *Life* magazine—now you act like you're the father welcoming home the prodigal son."

Sinclair scowled at Spain. He was a crusty sort, tenacious and virtually impervious to insults. "Speaking of prodigals, Morton, you'd better keep an eye on your wife."

"What do you mean?" Spain jerked his head around in the direction Sinclair had nodded.

Angela stood beneath a red-white-and-blue sign proclaiming, "Ben Logan for State Senator—He's One of Us!" She gazed up into the face of Clay McCain with rapt fascination as she engaged him in animated conversation.

"Why she's just talking to Clayton," Spain proclaimed as though he had explained a riddle to Sinclair. "What in the world is wrong with that?"

Sinclair glanced at the young couple, then gave Spain a knowing smile. "I didn't say anything was wrong, did I?" he called over his shoulder as he turned and walked toward the speaker's platform.

Spain hurried over to his wife. "I wish you'd let me know before you take off like that, Angela. I feel like I'm trying to keep up with a child."

"Oh, don't be so bothersome, Morton," Angela shot back. "You expect me to stand there and let Mayor Sinclair bore me to death? I'm finding out all about Clay's big contract with the Boston Red Sox."

"When did this happen?"

Clay stuffed his hands into his blue letter jacket, smiling self-consciously. "It hasn't happened, Mr. Spain. I was just telling Ang—uh, Mrs. Spain that one of the Boston scouts had come down last year to look at me."

"Yes, well, I'm sure that's all very interesting, Clayton," Spain muttered. "C'mon, dear, let's find a good spot before they're all taken."

"This one's just fine with me." Angela smiled brightly, stepping a shade closer to Clay.

Spain took her firmly by the arm, leading her away. "C'mon, I think I see a better place."

"There goes trouble just trying to find the right place to happen."

Clay turned around to see J.T. Dickerson walking up behind him. He had shaved and combed his hair and wore a pinstriped suit coat over his gray Harvard sweat shirt.

"Hey, J.T. Glad you could make it."

J.T. stared at Spain as he led his wife hurriedly away. "You better watch that one."

"Angela?"

"It's just a matter of time before ol' Morton gets his belly full of her running around."

"Maybe she's just being friendly. Probably gets tired of hanging around that big house all the time." Clay felt a need to defend Angela in spite of all the gossip.

"I'm afraid she's going to get friendly one time too many," J.T. spoke in a somber tone. "Just hope you aren't around when it happens, son."

"Don't worry about that," Clay answered not quite sincerely. "She's too old for me."

J.T. shook his head slowly. "Yep, I expect she's nearly senile by now. Must be twenty-one at least—maybe even twenty-two."

5

THE CLEAR LIGHT
OF OCTOBER

*I*t was the first autumn after the war began and 42 percent of American households had telephones. Inflation and unemployment registered exactly the same figure: 4.7 percent. A Harris tweed coat cost $26.95, and you could go into almost any department store and buy a washable rayon dress for $3.95.

Nine hundred and twenty-five AM radio stations around the country broadcast General Douglas MacArthur proclaiming: "The President of the United States ordered me to break through the Japanese lines and proceed from Corregidor to Australia for the purpose of organizing the American offense against Japan. . . . I came through and I shall return."

Americans also listened to programs like "People Are Funny" with Art Linkletter and "Fibber McGee and Molly" and heard Walter Winchell bring them the latest news. "Don't Sit Under the Apple Tree" by the Andrew Sisters, "Paper Doll" by the Mills Brothers, and "I've Got a Gal in Kalamazoo" by Glenn Miller, who also received the first gold record for "Chattanooga Choo Choo," were among the most popular tunes.

Liberty's young men departed with alarming regularity now for cities, countries and islands they had never heard of before at the beckon of their Uncle Sam. The railway station bustled with families bidding farewell to their sons and daughters, some of whom they would never see again.

The battle still raged for Guadalcanal at places like Ironbottom Sound, the Tenaru River, and "Bloody Ridge." Montgomery was about to launch his attack against Rommel's force at El Alamein. In the North Atlantic, the Allied shipping losses to the wolf packs reached a half-million tons per month.

* * *

Morton Spain knotted his red-and-gray-striped tie in a perfect four-in-hand and brushed his thin hair across his head for the final time before he walked down the hall to the kitchen. Taylor, still sleep-rumpled and drowsy, stood at the stove frying bacon. He wore jeans and a T-shirt and his acne showed as dull red blotches in the glare of the fluorescent lighting.

"Morning, son," Spain greeted him, painfully aware of the skin condition that even the best specialists in Atlanta were unable to treat. "You sure got things smelling good in here. I didn't know you could cook."

"A little something I picked up at college," Taylor grinned, brushing his dark hair back from his face.

Spain poured coffee and sat down at the table, opening the morning paper. "Says here that Gene Autry enlisted in the service. With him and Jimmy Stewart both in there, this war oughta be over in six months' time."

"I hear all four of the president's sons are in the armed forces." Taylor forked the bacon onto a small platter and reached for the eggs that sat in a white bowl on the counter. "You still eat your eggs straight up?"

"Yep."

Taylor broke two eggs into the grease that hissed and popped in the skillet. Turning down the burner, he moved them gently around with the spatula, splashing grease over their tops. "Dad . . ."

Spain stopped reading and stared over it at his son. "What is it, son?"

"I think I'm going to leave college and join up."

"Nonsense. You've only got two years left." Spain's voice held the courtroom authority he had practiced for years to perfect. "When you graduate, you can go in as an officer."

Taylor shoveled the eggs onto a plate and set it on the table. Staring down at his father, he spoke with hesitation, "Dad, I-I can't take it around here anymore."

Spain looked up from his eggs, the salt shaker held out in one hand. "What are you talking about? This is your home. I know it hasn't been easy on you and Rae since your mother died, but Angela—"

"That's exactly it—Angela." Taylor went back to the stove and broke two more eggs into the skillet.

"What has she done to you?"

Taylor turned around, shaking his head slowly. "Nothing. It's what she's done—is doing to you."

Spain had tried to bury his doubts about Angela—about their marriage, but there were times such as now when was forced to confront them. He picked up the newspaper and tried to concentrate on an editorial, then slapped it back on the table.

"You must have wondered why Rae married so quickly?" Taylor turned back to the stove, speaking in a more subdued voice now. "She'd only known Bill for a month. It was to get away from this house—this town."

Spain sighed, his shoulders slumping. "The two of you think I'm just an old fool."

Taylor turned off the burner and pulled a chair up next to his father. "No, Dad. I could never think that about you. I think you were lonely after Mama died. You just happened to run into the wrong woman."

"She's just so *young*, Taylor." Spain turned his anguished eyes on his son. "Give her some time. She'll settle down and things will be just fine."

"It's been four years, Dad."

Spain thought of the terrible grief he suffered after his wife's death and of how his whole world had changed after he had met Angela. He remembered those months when he had courted her and the envious looks he got from the men when he would take her to church or to a town picnic or simply for a stroll along the streets on a warm summer evening.

Lately, he found himself thinking more and more about those days and about the first few months of his marriage, which were the happiest of his life since he had been a young man. He dwelt on those fleeting times because for more than three years now there had been precious few times when he had had any joy or even peace of mind in his marriage.

"I know how long it's been, but there's still time for things to get better," Spain pleaded for understanding from his son. "They just *have* to."

Taylor saw that there was no sense in pursuing the matter any further. His father was hopelessly and senselessly in love with Angela. "Maybe you're right, Dad."

Spain brightened. "Certainly I'm right. Now you forget about this joining the Army business and get your mind back on your studies."

"Sure, Dad." Taylor knew that he would be coming back home very little now, if at all, and he still hadn't ruled out the idea of joining the service. One thing he was certain of—he had had all he could take of the crude remarks about his stepmother from the men in town.

Taylor took his plate and a cup of coffee and sat down at the table. "I never see you go to breakfast anymore down at the Liberty Hotel. You used to love going there to get the day started off with all your buddies."

Spain cleared his throat. "Well, I guess anything gets old after a while, and that was a habit for years and years." Spain could almost hear the chuckles from his friends as he would enter the restaurant each morning. Only twice did he actually hear any gossip about Angela, but it eventually reached the point when any time someone would laugh, he thought it was at his expense. Finally the day came when he could face it no longer, and the "habit of years" that he had dearly loved was over.

After Taylor had dressed and left to drive back to school, Spain sat in a metal glider on the flagstone terrace behind his house and enjoyed the warmth of Indian summer. The morning breeze moved through the willow limbs at the end of the terrace, creating a shifting pattern of sunlight and shade on the stones below. Gazing over the expanse of lawn, he stared at the rainbow haze hovering in the mist of the water sprinklers.

At the back of the property, Spain noticed Amos, his sixty-year-old Negro groundskeeper as he trimmed the hedge that surrounded the grounds. He wore his usual khakis and brogans and worked with his usual calm and deliberate pace that he would keep up all day long. Although he had employed Amos for almost twenty years, Spain suddenly realized that he knew virtually nothing about the man.

He's got a wife and three children—I think. I don't even know where he lives. Spain was so used to seeing his property perfectly manicured that the grounds might have been a painting that someone replaced with the changing of the seasons. *I'll have to make it a point to talk to him some day. But now I'll be late for court if I don't hurry.*

* * *

"Don't forget to take the package to the depot. Taylor needs that book as a reference for his pre-law exams." Morton Spain spoke to Angela from the driver's seat of his idling black Cadillac.

Angela stood under the back portico of their home, pulling her quilted housecoat about her against the morning chill. "I'll drop it off on my way to Hightower's. I want to buy some Halloween decorations for the house."

"That's for children, Angela. There's only the two of us here now."

"I don't care, Morton," Angela pouted. "I never had any as a child. Taylor and Rae would have made fun of me, but they're gone now."

Spain never ceased to be amazed at Angela's chronic and erratic metamorphoses from woman to child and back to woman again. "If it makes you happy."

Angela smiled at her tiny victory. "What time will you be back from Atlanta?"

"Probably not until two or three in the morning. You never know how long a hearing like this will last." Spain noticed with a gnawing sense of unease how his wife tried to conceal her delight at the prospect of his being away for so long. "I may just spend the night."

Angela walked over to the car and kissed him lightly on the cheek. "Poor dear! Don't work too hard."

"What do you do to occupy your time while I'm away on these trips, Angela?" Morton seemed unable to stop himself from asking the same tired question, the one that seemed to have become more riddle than question judging by Angela's inability to give him a sensible answer.

"Oh, you know. Polish my nails, listen to the radio, read a magazine."

"You need to develop some interests, hobbies—something. You must be bored to death."

"No, I'm not." Angela frowned.

"I'm only thinking of you, Angela," Spain reassured her. "I don't want you wasting your life."

Angela's face brightened. "How could you say I'm wasting my life when I'm married to you?"

Spain stared into Angela's violet eyes, disturbed at the peculiar cast he saw in them. Then without even attempting to return her smile, he drove away.

* * *

Angela drove to the depot along the quiet midmorning streets. Huge oaks and elms grew in front of the nineteenth-century houses, tall and gabled and white with gray wraparound porches. Painted with autumn colors of red and rust and copper, the ancient trees blazed brilliantly in the clear light of October. She loved this time of year with its crisp, dry air and the scent of smoke from chimneys and wood-burning stoves that many people, even in town, still cooked on.

Pulling into the depot parking lot, Angela saw people scattered along the platform near the train. Young men in uniform seemed to be at the center of each group. Old women and young women, some with tears glistening in their eyes, clung to their men-at-arms. There was an occasional handshake or slap on the back from fathers or brothers who, for the most part, hung back on the edges of the little groups.

Angela hurried up the front steps of the station, entered through the front glass doors, and took her package over to the counter.

Stanley Adams, the stationmaster, a short plump man with wire spectacles, waddled over to Angela from his desk. "What can I do for you, Mrs. Spain?"

Since the first time she had seen him, Angela had thought Adams looked like Santa Claus without a beard, even wearing his black uniform with its flat-crowned and shiny-billed hat. "I need to send this to Taylor—something important for his studies. His daddy will kill me if it isn't on today's train."

"Oh, I doubt that, Mrs. Spain." Adams peered at Angela over the rims of his spectacles. "I'll bet your husband never even gets mad at you."

Angela smiled and gave Adams a five-dollar bill. She waited for her change while he stamped the package and placed it on the cart with the other mail.

"Hello, Angela. My, don't you look lovely today." Lila Kronen, wearing a tan jacket over her brown sweater and slacks, stood next to the counter. Her smile radiated warmth as surely as the huge pot-bellied stove standing in the center of the station waiting room.

Angela turned to look at the older woman she had met at a luncheon at the country club. She had since seen her at several other functions and had become fond of her. "Why, thank you, Lila," she replied, glancing down at her burnt-orange dress. "Just something from last year."

"How's Morton?"

"He's fine. Over in Atlanta today on business."

"Here you are." Adams handed Angela her change.

"Thank you. Are you sure it'll go out today?"

"Guaranteed."

"How are things going with your newspaper, Lila?" Angela had heard that Dobe Jackson, who owned the *Liberty Herald,* was not pleased at all at the prospect of competition.

"Slowly I'm afraid," Lila admitted. "I'm here to pick up a part for the press. Henry says that sitting idle all that time was the worst thing that could have happened to it."

Angela glanced over at the three tables Adams had placed near the windows that looked over the station platform. With all the wartime traffic, he had decided to make a little extra money for himself by selling coffee. "If you're not in a hurry, we could have some coffee."

"They haven't unloaded the mail yet, Mrs. Kronen," Adams volunteered.

"Fine, " Lila smiled.

They seated themselves while Mr. Adams brought two steaming white mugs of coffee and placed them on the table. Lila handed him a dollar.

"I'll be right back with your change."

"You keep it, Mr. Adams," Angela said with a flick of her painted nails. "This looks like great coffee."

"A dollar for two dime cups? It ain't that great." Adams stared at the dollar bill as he went back to his counter.

"When do you think you'll get your first newspaper out, Lila?" Angela asked as she poured cream into her coffee.

"You sound like Henry." Lila glanced out at the people milling about on the platform. "It's been almost six months and I haven't been able to sell one ad yet. Maybe a handful of people have said they'd take subscriptions. Old habits die hard and everyone here is so used to the *Herald* that they're skeptical of anything else. I'll probably have to finance the first few issues with my own money until the good citizens of Liberty can see what they're going to get for their dimes."

"Well, you can put the Spain household down for a subscription," Angela beamed. "Morton says he's getting tired of Dobe Jackson's editorials condemning every German and Japanese on the face of the earth."

"I've noticed he seems to have some kind of fixation on the subject."

Angela had enjoyed the few conversations she had had with Lila and this one was no exception. Somehow, and she was unable to comprehend why, Lila made her feel like she was somebody special. "It's not like everybody in the whole country doesn't already know why we're fighting this war—he has to continually remind us like he's the only true-blue American and it's his duty to convert the rest of us. And even worse, the Japanese- and German-Americans had nothing at all to do with starting it."

"I should hope not," Lila agreed readily. "I was born in Germany, and I consider myself as loyal an American as there is in this country."

"I didn't know you were German."

"Oh, I don't remember anything about the country. I was only six months old when our family came here."

Angela chinked her teaspoon lightly on the side of her mug, her face thoughtful, then as if no one had ever thought of it before she proclaimed, "We all came over here from somewhere else, didn't we? I mean our families did even if we didn't."

Lila smiled at Angela's revelation. "That's right. And it's

thinking like Dobe Jackson's that allowed a man like Adolph Hitler to come to power."

"What do you mean?"

"I mean blaming a whole class or race of people—like the Jews—for a country's problems. It unites people against an alleged common enemy, plays on their fears like Jackson's trying to do with the Japanese and Germans who are as American as anyone else. And in his case, it sells newspapers for him."

"I think you might have some problems with Mr. Jackson before this war's over, Lila."

"I expect you're right, but I've had problems before." Lila sipped her coffee and stared at Angela, her brow furrowed in concentration. "We can't let that kind of thinking go unchecked in this country. It'll be the end of us if we do."

"You mean treating the Japanese here the same as the Japanese who started the war?"

"I guess I mean condemning any group of people for injustices they had nothing to do with." Lila felt like Angela was sometimes more her student than her friend and found herself enjoying the role of teacher. "For instance, slavery was a terrible blight on this country. But would you condemn every white person alive for its existence? It was abolished eighty years ago. No one alive now ever owned slaves, and only a small percentage did before its death.

"The sane thing to do is to right the injustices that still exist with the Negroes today. Give them the same freedoms and opportunities that everyone else has. What purpose would it serve to judge people now for the wrongs that happened before they were even born?

"I for one refuse to accept blame for what my forebears did generations before I came into existence." Lila noticed the puzzled expression on Angela's face. "I do tend to ramble on, don't I? Just tell me to hush when that happens."

"Oh, no." Angela smiled. "I don't have conversations like this with anyone else but you, Lila. It's certainly interesting for me and—different."

Lila shook her head slowly. "I guess I'm just frustrated that a mean-spirited man like Adolph Hitler can cause so much heartache and suffering in the world. I believe that every little petty tyrant like him that thrives on an agenda of bigotry and fear is nothing but a coward—inside they're just frightened little boys who have no abilities, nothing to offer the world, so they tap in somehow to hatred and jealousy, the absolute worst qualities of people, and manipulate them for their own despicable ends. Why do we even listen to them?" Lila stopped suddenly, placing her hand over her mouth. "I did it again, didn't I? Guess I'd better get my newspaper going so I can put all this in print. Maybe then I'll stop boring people to death."

Angela found herself staring in rapt fascination at Lila as she spoke so fervently. "I don't think you're boring. I do think you probably wouldn't be welcomed back to Germany though—not for a while anyway."

"You're probably right." Lila laughed.

Angela glanced out the window. "Look! We started all this speaking about Dobe Jackson, and there comes his daughter, Diane, with Clay McCain."

"J.T. told me Clay had joined the Marines."

"Poor Diane. Her daddy's been against her seeing Clay, and now he's off to fight with the Marines. I guess there are stories like that all over the country."

Lila had become intrigued. "What's Jackson got against Clay? I hear he's a fine boy."

"Fine, but poor," Angela said matter-of-factly. "It's a quality Dobe finds—distasteful. See, hanging around with you is helping my vocabulary."

"But he's going to sign with Boston, isn't he? He'll have plenty of money then."

"That's not sure enough for ol' Dobe, especially with the war on," Angela explained, staring at Clay's broad shoulders and slim hips as he stood talking with Diane and his parents. "If I weren't married . . ."

Lila gave Angela a knowing frown. "What's Dobe's idea of the ideal mate for his daughter?"

"Probably somebody like Keith Demerie." Angela made a face when she said it. "He's a decent looking-boy, but he won't do a thing without asking his daddy first. I think all Dobe cares about is the fact that Tyson Demerie is a senator and could help him out politically."

"You're giving me quite an education on the town, Angela.

Maybe it'll come in handy if I ever get this newspaper going. It helps to know the competition." Lila watched Clay kiss his mother and shake hands with his father. Then she saw Diane follow him over to the edge of the platform where he took her in his arms and kissed her then hopped aboard the train just as the engine's steam whistle gave a loud blast.

"I sure hope Clay makes it back all right," Angela said softly, staring at the line of green Pullman cars lurching out of the station. "He's such a nice boy."

Lila gazed out the window. Clay's mother had buried her face against her husband's shoulder. "They're all nice boys, Angela."

"I'd hate to be a man," Angela remarked, as though realizing for the first time the terrible uncertainty of war and the even more terrible finality of death. "I don't think I'd have the courage to fight."

"Most of us find the courage to do what we have to do—one way or the other. It's either that or give up on life," Lila observed. "Well, I guess I'll get back to work. I see Mr. Adams has the mail unloaded. You coming?"

Angela had noticed a sailor crossing the platform in his dress blues, carrying a duffel bag on his shoulders. He was slim and well built with short dark hair and a clean profile. Something about him made Angela think that her long-dead brother would have grown up to look something like he did. It never occurred to her that the young man bore a marked resemblance to the picture of her father that she kept next to her bed.

"Are you leaving, Angela?"

"What? Oh, sorry I didn't hear you." Angela glanced again at the sailor who was walking toward the door leading into the station with that overconfident tread common to young healthy men. "Not just now. I think I'll have another cup of coffee, maybe talk to Mr. Adams a few minutes." Lila watched as the sailor entered the station and walked over to speak with the stationmaster. He glanced back over his shoulder toward Angela.

"We'll have to do this again soon, Angela." Lila stood up to leave.

"I'd love to." Angela forced her gaze back to Lila. "I really enjoy being with you, Lila. I hope we can remain friends. There aren't many people I can talk to."

Lila picked up her package, waved goodbye to Angela, and left the station by the front door. As she walked across to her car, she glanced back into the station through the tall windows. Smiling down at Angela, the young sailor stood next to the chair Lila had just left.

6

CASUALTY OF WAR

"Wayne Perez," the young sailor volunteered, flashing a mouthful of white teeth in his deeply tanned face. "Mind if I join you?"

Angela knew he would be joining her as soon as she had glanced at him over her shoulder and saw his eyebrows raise slightly. She hesitated now, just enough to make him shift about uneasily, twirling his white cap on the forefinger of his left hand. "Well, I don't usually talk to strangers, but since you're in uniform I guess it won't hurt to have a cup of coffee with you."

"You're sure I won't be disturbing you?" Perez asked in an excess of politeness.

Angela merely pointed a red fingernail at her empty coffee mug.

"Sure thing," Perez said quickly and dropped his duffel bag against the wall next to his chair. Placing his own mug on the table, he hurried over to the counter with Angela's.

When he returned with the coffee, Perez took his seat, gazing in silence at the almost luminous glow of Angela's skin as the pale light through the window touched it. He dumped four spoonfuls of sugar into his mug, spilling a large portion of it on the table.

Angela loved to play the game. She stared disinterestedly out the window at the station platform, empty now except for a porter wearing overalls, a battered felt hat, and a red plaid shirt, who wheeled a cart back to its place near the loading dock.

Perez couldn't believe his good fortune, but he felt pressured to say something before this elegantly dressed and obviously well-off woman became bored with him and walked forever out of his life. "I'm from El Paso."

Angela turned her head slowly in his direction. "Sounds Spanish. Are you Spanish, Mr. Perez?"

"Mr. Perez? I haven't heard that three times in my whole life. Call me Wayne." Perez couldn't decide whether she was putting him on or not.

"Well, are you?"

"Am I what? Oh, sure! I don't speak the language often though. Papa said if we want to be good Americans we should speak English."

"He's probably right."

"By the way, I didn't get your name."

"English."

"English?"

"Angela English."

"Oh." Perez sipped his coffee, making a slurping sound in his nervousness.

Angela smiled into her white mug.

"Excuse me. This is my first time away from home—I guess I'm a little nervous."

"How old are you?" Angela stared straight into Perez's dark eyes.

Perez set his mug on the table, glancing over at the counter as though Adams could somehow give him more confidence. "Almost eighteen."

"Really? You look *much* older." Angela had decided to end the "make them uncomfortable first" stage of this destined-to-be-brief relationship.

"Papa said there's nothing like going into the service to turn a boy into a man." Perez sat up a little straighter in the wire-backed chair. "He still calls me his boy, though. You know how papas are about their children."

Angela thought of her own father, holding his little cardboard suitcase and squinting into the sun the morning he disappeared forever from her life. She remembered that he walked away without even a glance in her direction. For three years or more she had looked time and again at that same spot in the road, hope slowly fading that he would someday reappear where she had seen him last. "Yes. They're all the same, aren't they?"

"You still live with your family?" Perez glanced down at Angela's ring finger.

His glance wasn't wasted on Angela. She thought of her wedding ring and the three carat engagement ring resting in the bottom of her purse. "Yes. I think my daddy would just die if I tried to move out of the house. He doesn't want me to leave home even for a few days. We live over in Atlanta. I'm just visiting my aunt here in Liberty."

"I'm on my way to New Jersey now. I just finished boot camp in San Diego." Perez still couldn't figure out why Angela had any interest in him, but he was starting to relax and enjoy himself. "They gave me a month's liberty first. My mother sure didn't want me to leave when it was up."

"Why did you pick the Navy?"

"Oh, that was my uncle's idea—my papa's oldest brother. He's a drill instructor at boot camp in San Diego." Perez thought of his uncle sitting at their family's kitchen table in the little three-room apartment in El Paso and of how as a ten-year-old boy he wanted more than anything else to be like him—to wear a real Navy uniform and sail around the world to places he could only read about in books.

He thought as well of how he had dreaded the prospect of ending up like his own father, old beyond his years, with a sun-burned and craggy face and hands like gnarled brown wood from twelve-hour days in the elements, mixing and carrying mortar for the bricklayers on construction jobs. "What does your papa do for a living?" he asked Angela.

"Oh, he's a lawyer." As always, Angela was beginning to feel more like the person she had begun to create with her words than the person she actually was. "He gets so busy sometimes we hardly ever see him. But then he'll just shut everything down, cancel all his appointments—won't even take calls from judges—and we have barbecues in the back yard, go to movies, and sometimes stay at our cabin out on the lake."

Perez was becoming more and more confused about why Angela would want to spend any time with him. "I never even saw a lake till I joined the Navy."

"How long have you got?" Angela had decided that she would be safe with Perez and now wanted to spend as little time as possible in the public eye.

"Excuse me?"

"When do you have to leave?" Angela asked, a hint of irritation in her voice.

Perez glanced at the big schoolhouse clock above Adams' desk. Things were moving so fast he found himself in a kind of daze. "My train leaves at five-thirty. That gives me six-and-a-half hours."

"Why don't we go somewhere and have a drink—maybe listen to some music?"

Perez couldn't believe his good fortune. He felt like a kid on his way to the circus. "I'd really like that!" Pushing his chair back, he noticed the frown on Angela's face.

Angela leaned over the table, whispering, "Wait till I'm gone. My aunt wouldn't understand my meeting you like this—she's kind of old fashioned. She doesn't understand that we have to keep up the morale of our fighting men."

"Oh." Perez looked around the empty station waiting room, then gave Adams a glance. "You think he'd tell her about us?"

"They're good friends," Angela nodded, "and this isn't a very big town."

Perez picked up his empty coffee mug, turning it up as though he were drinking.

Angela slung the strap of her brown leather purse around her shoulder. "Wait ten minutes after I'm gone, then walk four blocks west. Wait for me on the corner where the gravel road intersects this street."

Perez, trying painfully to look nonchalant, nodded his head to each of Angela's instructions.

"You can leave your bag with Mr. Adams. Tell him you just want to walk around and see a little of the town." Standing up, Angela spoke a little too loudly, "Nice meeting you. You take care of yourself now."

"You too," Perez replied, grinning broadly at Angela then over at Adams. "Tell your papa I said he raised a fine daughter. Maybe I'll see you sometime after the war's over."

* * *

He wouldn't have noticed it at all as he drove past Slick Willie's Tavern except that it looked so out of place. Three muddy log trucks, their cabs bashed and dented from years of rough service in the woods, a handful of Model T's, and thirties vintage Chevrolets decorated the rutted gravel parking lot. Several horses, still harnessed to their wood-sided wagons, stood tied to trees at the edge of the woods.

Angela's black LaSalle had been backed carefully behind the tavern, but its shiny grill glinted in the sunlight, catching Spain's eye as he headed eagerly back toward home, grateful for the opportunity to spend the rest of the day with his wife.

Spain's Cadillac had broken down fifty miles outside of Liberty. Calling the courthouse in Atlanta from a service station while his car was being repaired to inform them of his delay, he had learned that the hearing had been postponed; the judge had suffered a heart attack on the way to the courthouse.

With the glimpse of Angela's car parked at that infamous tavern, the years of suspicion and doubt seemed to weigh down on Spain so heavily and so suddenly that he felt himself in danger of also having a heart attack. After driving five miles, his eyes clouded with the pain that seemed to sweep over him from deep in his chest, he pulled into a gravel drive with a leaning mailbox, backed onto the highway, and drove back the way he had come.

*　*　*

The muted ticking of the clock on the dashboard of Spain's Cadillac had been the only companion for his solitary vigil. When he glanced at it, it told him he had been sitting in the parking lot at the edge of the woods for an hour and twenty-five minutes. Several men, one or two in the company of heavily rouged and lightly dressed women, had stared at him as they left the tavern, clinging roughly to each other.

At one point a young sailor had walked from the front door to Angela's car and taken an overnight bag out of the trunk. He had then climbed the wooden steps up to the five rooms located on a bluff behind the tavern. He went into room number four, came back out without the bag, and returned to the tavern.

After he had seen the sailor, Spain's eyes became glazed and vacant, almost as though an opaque film had been slowly drawn over them. The pain in his chest intensified as unbearable pictures flickered at the back of his mind like worn-out copies of ancient silent films. His head seemed filled with the suppressed laughter of his friends when he passed their tables in the restaurant or encountered them on the street.

Spain recalled the day his son was born. He had gazed down at him in his mother's arms in the white bed of the white hospital room. He remembered that his wife had been the same age as Angela on that long ago day.

A man in greasy overalls, his eyes red and puffy from drink, staggered over to the car window, startling Spain from his reverie. He stood wobbly and glassy-eyed, motioning for Spain to roll his window down. "Name's Grogan. You need some hep?" he asked, slurring his words.

Spain stared up at the man, shook his head, and rolled the window back up.

Grogan took four steps sideways, reached for an imaginary object in front of him and fell backward against the base of a pine tree. Struggling to his knees, he vomited onto the carpet of pine needles, his whole body retching with the effort. With a deep sigh, he fell onto his back and lay there, barely breathing, his eyes rolled back in his head.

Spain glanced out the window at Grogan, then looked away into his past. Startled by a sudden peal of thunder, he watched as the first few raindrops splashed on the hood of his car. He felt he had been sitting there all his life.

Leaning over on the seat, he reached into the glove compartment and took out a nickel-plated revolver. He cradled the pistol in both hands as though it might try to escape. A smile came slowly to his face as though some revelation that had eluded him all his life had finally come into focus. While he stared out into the rain, the light in his eyes went out as suddenly as if someone had thrown a switch inside his head.

The rain began to fall in earnest, becoming a gray curtain between Spain and the tavern with its flickering pale blue neon sign. It drummed steadily on the roof of the car, rustling and hissing high above in the leaves of the trees.

Grogan lay undisturbed underneath the pine tree, his cheek pressed against the carpet of needles, his lips making a soft plopping sound as he expelled air.

* * *

Smoke hung in the stale air close to the ceiling and drifted in wispy clouds across the room. Most of the stools along the bar were occupied by men, the few tables scattered near the opposite side were filled with couples. Pabst Blue Ribbon, Chesterfield, and Lucky Strike signs hung in random patterns on the walls. A juke-box glowed softly at the back of the room.

In the center of the bare concrete floor, a short, stocky man in cowboy boots and a Western shirt danced with a thin woman in a flowered dress and high-heeled patent-leather shoes. A cigarette dangled between the fingers of her bony hand hanging across his shoulder.

As she watched the dancers, Angela felt as light and insubstantial as the smoke after her four whiskey sours. "You know what?" she asked.

"Whaa?" Perez, his eyelids drooping sleepily, tried to bring Angela into focus as he gazed across the table at her.

"You remind me a little of Tyrone Power."

Perez sat up, blinked slowly, and took a sip from his water-beaded bottle of Pabst. He started to speak, but his tongue refused to form the words.

"You drink much?" Angela was amused at the effect the beer was having on Perez. He reminded her more of a child pilfering from the cookie jar than a sailor out on the town.

Perez took a deep breath and spoke haltingly. "One time before. W-we had a leave . . . boot camp and they—they took me out to . . ."

"You know something else?" Angela felt like an older sister to Perez. She wished now that she hadn't rented a room for the two of them. "You look like you're about ten years old. Have you ever had a girlfriend before, Wayne?"

Perez gazed at Angela with a sleepy smile on his face. "S°—I mean, yes. I guess you could say that. Juanita. She lived next door." He pushed the bottle of beer away from him and propped his elbows on the table, supporting his face in both hands. "We went to the movies a couple of times. I don't know if that made her my girlfriend or not."

"That's sweet."

Perez nodded and sat back in his chair, still smiling dreamily at Angela.

Angela realized now that the whole thing was a big mistake on her part. She thought of how much she would have liked to have had a brother. "Maybe I should take you on back to the depot now. You don't want to miss your train."

The jukebox began to play Tommy Dorsey's smoothly sentimental version of "I'll Never Smile Again" with Frank Sinatra's vocals backed up by the Pied Pipers.

"Let's dance." Perez placed both hands on the table and tried to stand up. He immediately plopped back down into his chair. "Let's don't dance," he giggled.

Angela smiled affectionately at him. "C'mon, I've got to get you back to the station."

Perez leaned toward Angela, his face as placid as that of a sleeping child. "You know something—this may not be such a bad war after all."

"What do you mean?"

"If it wasn't for the war, I never would have met you." Perez took Angela's hand in both of his, patting it gently. "This is the nicest time of my life."

They were the last words he ever spoke.

Angela saw a hole open suddenly in Perez's face just above his left eyebrow—the muzzle blast almost deafened her. Perez's head jerked back as his body slowly slid down in the chair. A single drop like a crimson tear rolled slowly down his face, followed by a rush of blood.

Angela heard herself screaming and thought at first that it was someone else from some other place in the room. Putting her hand over her mouth, she watched Perez collapse onto the floor with that rubbery, insentient motion that only death can produce in the human body.

Scraping her chair back on the rough floor, Angela turned to stand up, stopping in horror. Morton Spain stood ten feet away from her. His dark suit and silk tie, ruined by the rain, clung to his bony frame. The top of his bald head shone in the dim light. The few strands of hair that normally covered it had become plastered to the side of his face.

Angela thought she could see her own death reflected in the

dark, bottomless depths of his eyes. *Oh, God! Don't let this happen now! I'm not ready to die!*

With his face twisted in anguish and rage, Spain pointed the revolver directly at Angela's breast. She watched a tiny curl of smoke wisp upward from the barrel, then it exploded with yellow flame as a searing pain shot through the outside of her right shoulder.

Angela felt the warm flow from her shoulder with her left hand as she stared again into her husband's eyes, absent now of all light. Spain took one step toward her and leveled the pistol. Then he hurtled sideways, his upper torso ripped and torn by the shotgun blast.

Standing shakily, Angela saw the bartender standing a few feet away, a sawed-off twelve gauge gripped tightly in his thick, hairy hands. Her vision began to go fuzzy as the tavern became a spinning blur of light and color and noise. Vague forms of men and women moved as though in slow motion toward the door, escaping the carnage.

Forcing her head downward, Angela stared at her husband's shattered body crumpled amid the cigarette butts and mud and his own blood. Near him lay Perez, his right arm twisted beneath his body, his visible left eye holding that long vacant stare into eternity.

The bartender wiped his right hand on his stained apron, walked over to Angela and took her by the arm. "You all right? Looks like he grazed your shoulder."

Angela stared into the man's tiny brown eyes, set deep into his fleshy face. She opened her mouth to speak, then the darkness bore down on her with a smothering pressure and she fell down, down into a bottomless well where the wind howled about her in the choking blackness.

* * *

The cold October light created a patchwork of sunshine and shade as it cast shadows from the tall and ancient tombstones across the leaf-strewn ground of the cemetery. In the top of a scarlet sweet gum tree, a mockingbird sang to celebrate the last good days before the onset of winter.

Angela didn't hear the bird's song or see the bright plumage of the tree as she sat in one the twelve velvet-covered chairs next to her husband's grave. None of the other eleven had been occupied during the service. Taylor and Rae refused to sit with their father's widow, and the other family members had taken their cue from them.

When the service ended, the crowd, most clad in black, dispersed into small family groups, walking across the cemetery toward their cars. Occasionally one or two would stop at a gravesite and speak in low voices. Engines roared or sputtered to life, tires crunched across the gravel drive, and conversations resumed their normal levels as the speakers reached the accepted distance from the deceased.

Still Angela sat with her head bowed, the black hat and veil covering her red and swollen eyes. Her right arm hung across her breast in a sling. She stared at her left shoe, its high heel and thin black sole caked with red mud where she had walked too close to the open grave.

Thad Majors bade farewell to the last of the funeral crowd, most of whom belonged to his congregation, and walked back to the gravesite. He had a crinkly smile that reminded most people of Roy Rogers, and he had pastored the First Baptist Church of Liberty, Georgia, for thirty-two years. Placing his hand gently on Angela's shoulder, he spoke with genuine tenderness. "Is there anything I can do for you, Mrs. Spain?"

Angela merely shook her head.

"Are you sure?" Majors continued, knowing that she had no family left in town. "You're more than welcome to come and stay at our house for a while."

Angela gazed up into Majors's open and honest face. "No, thank you. You're very kind."

"Well, I'll be going then." Majors glanced down the hill at the chauffeured limousine, idling in the driveway. "I'll be by to check on you. You call if you need anything."

Angela nodded and shook his hand.

"I'll be praying for you, Mrs. Spain." Majors turned and followed his shadow down to his car.

Angela heard someone sit down in the chair next to her and felt a soft hand press gently on her gloved one. Turning, she saw Lila Kronen and her presence seemed to Angela to make the day almost bearable.

"You mustn't sit here any longer. There's nothing left to do." Lila took her hand, urging her to her feet.

The two women walked together to the waiting limousine where the driver opened the door for Angela.

"Take her directly home. I'll follow in my car."

When they reached the house, Angela walked woodenly up the back steps from the portico and down the long hall to the huge living room with its heavy antique furniture and tapestry rugs. She sat down on a plush sofa, staring out through the tall windows at the long expanse of front yard.

Lila knew that any words of comfort would be useless at this time. She took off Angela's hat and shoes, lifting her legs up on the sofa. Then she went into the kitchen, made a pot of tea, and brought it to the living room. With some effort, she was able to get Angela to drink most of a cup.

A bright rectangle of sunlight moved slowly across the gleaming hardwood floor as Lila sat with Angela through the afternoon. Finally, as the pale gold light faded to gray, Angela leaned over and fell into a deathlike sleep with her head in Lila's lap. Lila hummed softly to her, stroking her hair and watching the stars through the windows as they winked on one by one in the vast purple dome of the sky.

7

AFTERMATH

*A*ngela thought the music was lovely when she first heard it, but the recording of "I'll Never Smile Again" on the jukebox continued to play over and over, louder and louder. She put her hands to her ears, but it didn't help. Glancing around, she found herself back in the tavern. The smoke, thick as heavy fog, burned her lungs. She found herself coughing, gasping for breath. Now the music had become nothing more than a high-pitched wailing sound laced with deep, horrible groans.

Struggling to stand up, Angela found that her arms and legs felt like they were made of lead, nothing but dead weight that she had no control over. She tried to scream, but no sound came from her open mouth.

With horror, she saw Perez sitting in his chair across the table from her. The gaping hole above his left eye was crusty with dried blood. It had streamed down the side of his face, pooling in the small hollow of his collar bone.

"I'm so sorry, Wayne." Angela's voice sounded cracked and dry, like that of a very old woman.

"You should have told me, Angela." Perez stared at her, his soft, dark eyes unbearably sad. "I didn't know. You should have told me."

Suddenly the concrete floor opened into a cavernous hole beneath her. She hurtled downward in a swirling maelstrom of wind and darkness and screams of unimaginable torment. Miles below, she could see light flickering in red and yellow waves across the bottom of a stony pit—smoke rose toward her in a black, malevolent cloud.

"Oh, God! Help me!" Angela sprang up from the dream, her body soaked in a cold sweat. Her breath came in ragged gasps as

she struggled up from the twisted sheets. She ran into her bathroom and stripped off the soaked nightgown. Adjusting the water
temperature to as hot as she could stand it, she stood under the
shower until she stopped shivering.

After toweling her hair dry, she dressed in jeans with a red
flannel shirt and penny loafers then went into the kitchen and
made tea. As she sat at the table sipping the hot liquid, the huge
rooms and expensive furnishings around her seemed more like a
vast tomb than a home. She felt almost like an ancient Egyptian
queen she had read about in one of the reference books in her
husband's library. She had been buried alive with pomp and cer-
emony and all her earthly treasures.

No longer able to stand the emptiness of the house—the dolor
of familiar surroundings had become her enemy—Angela grabbed
her black leather jacket from the clothes tree and ran down the back
steps of the portico to her car. She drove through the deserted
streets while the dashboard clock ticked off the fleeting minutes of
her life.

*   *   *

Angela found herself pulling into the parking lot of an all-
night cafe on the highway outside of town. A hand-lettered sign
above the door proclaimed: Smitty's—The Best Homemade Biscuits in the World. Paint flaked off the walls, and dust and grime
caked a row of windows across the front. A yellow cur, his hide
splotchy with mange, loped around from the deep shadows on the
side of the building at the sound of the automobile invading his
domain. A heavy chain jerked him up short before he had gone
twenty feet.

After waiting a few seconds to make sure the dog was securely
bound, Angela walked up the front steps and into the neon glare
inside, taking a seat at the end of the counter on a stool covered in
red vinyl.

Glancing around the nearly deserted cafe, she noticed a young
couple sitting close together in a booth across from her. Eating
hamburgers and greasy hash browns, they appeared as happy as if
they had been dining in the most elegant and expensive restaurant
in Atlanta.

The groom had unkempt brown hair and pimples. He wore a suit that had probably set him back five dollars. His bride, holding out her left hand every few minutes to admire her tiny gold band, wore a blue cotton dress and a heavy brown work coat. Freshly washed, her straight blond hair gleamed in the bright light.

"Hep you?"

Angela turned around quickly at the sound of the coarse voice. The man standing behind the counter wore a grease-stained apron over his ponderous belly. He sported several days' growth of dark stubble and his rheumy eyes squinted out from under bushy brows. A purple cobra, tattooed on his left bicep, entwined itself around a human skull.

She almost asked for tea, then glancing at her surroundings replied in a dry voice, "Coffee, please."

"It ain't fresh."

"That's OK."

The man waddled over to the coffee urn, drew a thick mug full and pushed it across the counter with coffee sloshing over the side. "Ten cents."

Angela fished a dime out of her purse, placing it in the man's pudgy hand.

"Holler loud if you want something else. I might be asleep." He disappeared into the back behind a curtain hanging over an open doorway.

"Oh, it's so purty. Where did you get the money to buy it?" The bride, still admiring her ring, spoke in a voice that was as much child as woman.

"Been saving fer a long, long time," the groom replied with obvious pride. "Nothing's too good fer my wife. You're jest as purty as a speckled puppy under a red wagon."

Angela heard giggling and a soft smacking sound as the bride expressed her appreciation for the compliment with a kiss. Then the sounds of eating resumed.

They can't be more than fifteen or sixteen. What chance do they have? Angela sipped her coffee, finding the cook to be a master of understatement with his choice of words, "It ain't fresh." *This stuff wasn't fresh yesterday.*

"This is a *good* hamburger." The bride seemed more than satisfied with her wedding supper.

"Best in this part of the country," the groom agreed readily. "We can come here after church on Sunday when the cotton crop's in and other times during the year when we got a little extra change in our pockets."

The bride smacked her lips and plopped ketchup onto her plate.

"Yessir. We gonna have us a real fine life. I ain't gonna haul pulpwood with Daddy for the rest of my life. No siree Bob. My cousin's got a body and fender shop in a little town just outside Atlanta."

"Atlanta? No kidding!" The bride's voice trilled with excitement.

"Yep. Course I gotta learn a little somethin' about the business first."

"You goin' to school?"

"Naw," the groom replied. "I got a mail-order book over to the house. It's got pitchers and everthang else you need to learn."

"Oh, I jes' can't wait!" The bride held her hamburger in midair, mayonnaise and beef fat dripped onto her plate as she spoke with youthful excitement of being newly married and moving to Atlanta. "I can see it all now. You and me living in one of them big ol' houses with a white picket fence and a brick sidewalk right up to the front porch—and maybe a young'un or two playing in the yard. I want a boy first. One jes' like his daddy."

The groom rubbed a particularly bothersome pimple on his cheek. "Now don't go puttin' the wagon in front of the mule. I gotta git my education first."

"You smart thang, you. You'll learn them books easy as pie," she assured him.

Looking back on her life, Angela wondered if she were ever that young and eager and full of wonder at what the future held, but could never recall such a time. She knew without a doubt that she had never shared such open and honest affection with anyone—not even her mother. She tried one more sip of coffee as the newlyweds finished their meal.

"I reckon we better git on back home," the groom said with a sly wink.

Taking her husband's hand and sliding out of the booth, the bride asked as she stared at the cluttered table. "Ain't you gonna leave him something?"

"Done paid him."

She glanced toward the door that led to the back of the cafe and raised up on tiptoe, almost whispering in his ear, "I mean something for a tip."

"Oh." The groom reached into his right front pocket and brought out two nickels and four pennies, holding them out in the flat of his hand. He thought of his next payday, which was almost two weeks away. *Well, I 'spect we won't need no money for a while anyhow.*

She smiled up at him, radiant as any other bride on her wedding night. "We only get married once, and besides he's a real nice feller."

"I reckon," the groom agreed. "Probably don't make much money either." Taking each coin in turn between his thumb and forefinger, he placed the two nickels and three pennies on the table. Glancing down at the remaining penny, he stuffed it back in his pocket. "I'll keep this 'un for luck."

The cook waddled out behind the counter and over to the jukebox at the end of the cafe. Dropping a nickel in, he punched two buttons and waved to the young couple. "How'd y'all like them burgers?"

"Jes' fine," they answered in unison, then laughed self-consciously.

"Y'all come back now."

They both nodded.

The cook walked back behind the counter and through the curtain.

Taking her husband's arm with both hands, the young bride sighed deeply and leaned on his shoulder as they walked together out into the night.

As Angela watched them leave, her eyes clouded with a longing she had felt all her life—for something unnamed and elusive. "I'll Never Smile Again" sounded from the jukebox, causing her to shudder involuntarily. Fishing some change from her purse, she dropped it on the counter and followed the young couple out the door. The chain clanked as the yellow dog reached the perimeter of his abbreviated world. This time he didn't bark.

Angela stood next to her car for a moment, watching the bride and groom as they walked across the parking lot onto the shoulder of the highway. Hearing a low rumbling growl, she glanced over at the dog. His yellow eyes gleamed in the wasted face.

In the dim light that filtered through the grimy windows of the cafe, Angela fumbled in her purse for the keys. She felt suddenly faint as she slumped onto the seat of the car. Taking a few deep breaths, she started the engine and jounced through a hole half full of water from last week's rain.

Angela passed the young couple as they turned onto a dirt lane that intersected the highway. As she glanced at them, the groom with his arm protectively around his bride, she found herself a victim of envy for what the young couple shared. A desperate need rose within her, an overpowering desire to lose herself somehow in that same shelter of affection.

Maybe someday I'll be a fine lady just like her. The young bride gazed at Angela with her own private longing as she drove past them.

The young man ruminated. *If I learn this body work stuff real good, I jes' might git to work on a car like that one day when we git to Atlanta. Wouldn't that be something?*

* * *

"Good morning, Lila." Angela walked into the reception room of the *Journal*, finding Lila sitting behind a desk banging away at a bulky black Royal typewriter. She wore a white blouse with ruffles at the throat.

Lila glanced up from her work, a yellow pencil clamped between her teeth. "Oh, hi, Angela. It's so good to see you! Where've you been keeping yourself?"

"At home mostly." Angela glanced around the room. It was freshly painted a pale green color. A wallpaper border in a dark green print ran beneath the walnut crown molding. Framed newspaper headlines hung on the walls, and in the far corner a coffee urn rested on a metal table with a white ceramic top. Several spoons stood upright in a tan mug of water next to a clear pint jar containing sugar.

Lila could see that Angela had lost weight by the way her wine-colored blouse and navy blue slacks hung on her small-boned frame. The black leather jacket looked a size too large. Her eyes were puffy and the skin beneath them had a bruised-looking cast from lack of sleep. "You need to get out of the house more, child. You're as pale as a lily."

"Maybe not *that* pale," Angela smiled.

Lila remembered the day of the funeral when she had spent the night with Angela, taking care of her almost as one would a small child. She had gone back to see her every day for a week afterward then gradually, as Angela appeared to be handling the tragedy better, Lila had thrown herself into the work at the *Journal*, which had lately occupied her time almost completely. "Are you doing all right now, Angela?"

"Oh, sure," Angela lied, thinking of the nights she spent driving around or simply walking the streets of Liberty, unable to bear the loneliness of her home.

"Why don't you come to church with me sometime?" Lila had asked her once before and had been promptly cut off. This time Angela showed some interest or at least wasn't inclined to hurt Lila's feelings. "It's nothing fancy, just a little wood-frame building out in the woods, but Pastor Shaw is a kind and godly man. You might even make some new friends."

"I-I don't know," Angela hesitated. "I haven't cared about being around people much lately."

Lila knew that the whole town was now aware of the circumstances of Morton Spain's death. As far as Angela's relationship with his family was concerned, this was dealt a death blow by the fact that his will had made her the beneficiary of the house and most of the money. For these reasons Spain's children and the remainder of the family had completely cut off contact with Angela. "Well, I guess I can understand that. You might find, though, that the people in our church are a little different from the crowd you've been around since your marriage."

"I don't know. Maybe later."

"No hurry."

"Anyway, I didn't come here to talk about me," Angela continued, happy to change the subject. "I wanted to see how you're doing with the newspaper."

"Well, Henry's been working like a miner getting the press ready and . . ."

"I don't mean that part of it," Angela interrupted, sitting down in a heavy wood chair. "I mean the nasty editorials Dobe Jackson's been writing."

"About his favorite subject you mean." Lila glanced furtively around the room as though expecting an intruder at any moment. "Every German and Japanese in the country is an enemy agent—a spy behind every bush."

"Well, since you came to town, he's just about quit blasting the Japanese. And the fact is, I've heard rumors about your being pro-German."

"So he's stooped to that level, has he? I guess he's more worried about competition than I had thought." Lila leaned back from her typewriter. "I guess I've been buried in this place so deeply I haven't paid much attention to the real world. Maybe it's time to fight back." Lila thought of the murmuring behind her back whenever she went grocery shopping or to the service station.

"I haven't seen many people myself lately, but Liberty's a small town and word gets around quickly. There's no way to prove that he started all this of course, but if he's thrown the name *Kronen* around in the right places, he can cause you some problems."

Lila stared out the window, tapping on the arm of her chair, a pensive look on her face. She eagerly awaited the chance to put her own views before the public.

"Have you sold many subscriptions yet?"

"Precious few," Lila replied, shaking her head. "And I don't even want to talk about the advertising. That's the real financial backbone of the newspaper business. Change doesn't come easily here in Liberty."

Angela felt Lila would just as soon not discuss her business. "Does J.T. still come around?"

"Pardon? Oh, yes he does occasionally. When the notion strikes him." Lila shook her head slowly, a half-smile lighting her face. "What a strange man. Maybe *unusual* would be a better word. He works like there's no tomorrow when he decides to—then disappears for weeks at a time."

Angela stared at Lila as if to speak, then looked away toward one of the framed headlines hanging behind her.

"Oh, I know about his drinking, Angela," Lila admitted,

thinking as she always did of the destruction it had wrought in J.T.'s life. "But there's more to it than that. It's like he's deathly afraid that he might get too close to someone."

"I've heard good and bad about J.T. Depends on who you talk to." Crossing her legs, Angela twisted her wedding ring around on her finger. She thought it ironic that she couldn't seem to bear having it off now that her husband was dead. "There was an old lady named Annie Sims—everybody called her Butcher Knife Annie— who lived in a dilapidated mansion just outside of town. She barely managed a living by collecting junk in a little red wagon she pulled around with her."

"I've heard about her. That was the family that was so rich at one time."

Angela nodded. "Annie had to raise her niece, Jordan. Her daddy just dropped the little girl off one night on his way to prison. I think she was about five years old at the time. They never heard from him again."

"I don't see what you're getting at."

"Well, if it hadn't been for J.T. helping them, they would never have made it. According to what I heard, he bought practically all of Jordan's clothes for the first few years after she started school." Angela's eyes seemed to darken briefly as though a fleeting shadow had passed by. "I guess he was the closest thing she had to a daddy when she was growing up."

"I hadn't heard that story yet," Lila replied, still amazed at the human capacity to spread negative gossip, forgetting about the good qualities a person might have. "I have heard all about J.T.'s wild escapades. Guess I haven't been here long enough for people to say anything good about him."

Angela slung the strap of her purse across her shoulder. "I won't keep you from your work any longer." She gazed directly into Lila's eyes. "I want to thank you again for all you did for me after Morton . . . I never would have made it if you hadn't been there to help me. I'll never be able to repay you for what you did for me when there was nobody else."

"I was more than happy to do it, Angela." Lila thought of the twenty-one childless years of her own marriage. "I never had any children of my own. I guess maybe I just considered you my little girl for a week or so."

Angela's eyes grew bright with tears. Standing up, she quickly brushed them away. "Well I'll never forget it."

Lila could only vaguely imagine the torment that followed Angela around like a scavenger waiting for her to be robbed of her last strength, her final vestige of a will to survive. Although she had spent her life with words, she couldn't seem to think of any that would fit the moment.

Angela had never let herself show emotion and was uncomfortable with the strong affection and gratitude she now felt. "I have to go," she called over her shoulder as she opened the door. "Come by when you have time."

"I will." Walking over to the half-glass door, Lila watched Angela hurry down the sidewalk to her car. "Poor child! There's only one way she'll ever have peace in her life again."

Lila returned to her typewriter, but the flow of words now seemed as solidly frozen as a Chicago puddle in February. She had long felt there was a purpose in the unexpected daily events of her life. Falling to her knees on the hard wooden floor, she bowed her head, groaning in her spirit for Angela Spain.

Outside, the December wind suddenly moaned through the eaves of the old building as though it were angry at the woman kneeling beyond its reach.

After a long while, Lila rose and seated herself at the typewriter. The words flowed again with the steady rhythmic tapping of the keys.

* * *

Angela drove for hours along the back roads outside of Liberty. Beyond the barbwire fences, the trees stood stark and leafless in the rolling pasture land. Their limbs in black and precise silhouette against the gray sky appeared to have been cut with tin snips. Cattle bunched close together, their backs against the wind, waiting for dusk and the call that would come ringing across the fields, summoning them to food and a warm barn.

Stopping on the shoulder of the road next to a bridge, Angela walked down to the bank of a small creek, sat on the trunk of a fallen sycamore, and unwrapped the ham sandwich she had brought with her from home that morning. She took a bite, chewing slowly. It tasted like sawdust, but she forced herself to swallow.

She stood up and walked to the edge of the six-foot bank, gazing down at the clear water that flowed slowly over a rocky bottom in the shallows. Bit by bit she pinched pieces of the sandwich off, tossing them into the creek. Red-ear bream, hand-sized and smaller, rose from the depths, striking viciously at the bits of food in flashes of color.

Angela sat down on the bank, watching the fish at their unexpected meal. When they had vanished into their fishy hiding places, she stared out across the brown pasture. The sun settled behind the distant hills, streaking the sky with shades of pink and violet and magenta.

When the light had faded and the sky moved toward a midnight shade, Angela suddenly felt the December cold seeping into her body. Rising from the damp grass, she went back to her car to resume her journey to nowhere until the gravel or blacktop surfaces in front of her became blurred by a weariness that would allow her to go home and drop off into a few hours of troubled sleep.

8

DRAWN TO THE LIGHT

*A*ngela noticed that the lights were still on in Ollie's Drug-store as she drove past. She glanced at the soft amber glow of the dashboard clock. *It's almost nine-thirty. I wonder why he's still open on Christmas Eve.*

The day had dawned mild and clear, but gradually a cold front had moved in from the northwest. By late afternoon, the sky was sealed with low gray clouds and the wind, tempered with an ironlike cold from the frozen wilds of Manitoba, drove the citizens of Liberty toward their fireplaces and woodburning stoves. A light rain began to fall at five o'clock and by seven the streets were deserted except for Moon Mullins making a few last minute deliveries of his bottled Christmas spirit.

Families gathered around their trees to celebrate the season with eggnog and fruitcake and presents. It was the one night of the year when children had gone to bed without threats of bodily harm. They tossed and turned and whispered in their beds, listening for the sound of sleigh bells. Although no one in memory had ever heard one, they all knew the sound would be so much nicer than that of church bells or those around the necks of cows. Morning seemed an eternity away.

* * *

For some reason unknown to her, Angela was drawn to the light inside Ollie's. Sleet ticked on her windshield as she pulled over to the curb beneath an ancient white oak. Its bare limbs wore a thin covering of ice, glittering in the pale amber light from the street lamps.

The cold cut through Angela's leather jacket and lavender

97

sweater as she left her car and walked the half-block to Ollie's. Entering to the sound of the bell on the glass-paneled door, she saw a solitary figure at the far end of the counter. He wore a jacket that was as dark as his hair. The man's head had been turned away from Angela as he looked toward the door that led to the back of the drugstore. The jukebox played Bing Crosby's biggest hit, "White Christmas."

Glancing around at the sound of the bell, Ben Logan smiled uneasily when he saw her step into the glare of the drugstore. "Merry Christmas, Angela."

As she walked slowly along the counter, Angela noticed that Ben wore his heavy wool uniform under his Navy pea jacket. His white cap lay on the stool next to him. "Merry Christmas, Ben. I should think you'd be home with your family."

"I had to pick up some more medicine for Mama. Seems like she just can't get well."

"Maybe your father's death is part of the reason," Angela suggested.

"I think you're right," Ben agreed. "She's always known that logging is dangerous business, but I guess you can never really be prepared for something like that to happen to your own family."

Wishing that she hadn't brought the subject up, Angela tried to lighten the mood. "Ollie didn't mind opening up on Christmas Eve? He should be considered for sainthood."

Ben smiled again, his teeth white against his face, which still held its tan from the hot Pacific sun and his days of cutting pulpwood with his father. "There are so many sick people calling him at home, he didn't have much choice about it if he wanted any peace on Christmas Day. He's filling the last prescriptions now. Said he's going to drop them off on his way home."

"I like that idea about sainthood, Angela." Ollie Caston leaned around the doorframe, his bow tie and neat brown crew cut giving the appearance of a much younger man. "Ben, I'm gonna be a little while finishing up back here. Why don't you fix you and Angela some hot chocolate?"

"Good idea." Ben walked around behind the counter, drew two mugs from the big urn, and nodded toward a booth. "Let's sit over there where it's comfortable."

Angela led the way to the last booth by the jukebox. She felt a

sense of guilt and shame at being with Ben, but she preferred anything to the emptiness of her house, with its creakings and
groanings in the night and the memories that seemed to come alive
and prowl its many rooms. "Ben, Rachel won't mind if you and I—
I mean . . ."

"No. I don't think so." Ben avoided the obvious question of
why Angela was alone on such a special night. Like most everyone
else in town, he had heard of the circumstances of her husband's
death. But unlike most of them, he had absolutely no inclination to
treat her as the town pariah.

"How do you like married life?"

Ben nodded his head slowly, a tender light coming to his clear
gray eyes. "Best thing that ever happened to me."

Angela sipped her chocolate. "I just heard about your wedding a couple of months ago."

"Well, Rachel's daddy married us at his house. I don't think it
made the society page."

Angela suddenly felt at ease with Ben. She couldn't explain it,
but he now seemed like a brother to her. "When do you have to go
back to your ship?"

Ben thought of the friends he had lost at Pearl Harbor. "I've
been asking for sea duty since they first told me I'd be traveling
around the country selling war bonds."

"What do they say?"

"That I'm worth more to the country here than if I went back
into combat." Ben pictured the air above Pearl Harbor alive with
Japanese fighters, heard the high, hard hammering precision of
the Mitsubishi engine as the Zero roared in, strafing the men
of the *Arizona* as they tried to flee their sinking ship. He could almost feel himself leaning hard into the shoulder rests of the 20
mm cannon, staring down the long clean length of its barrel—saw
again the heavy slugs raking the aircraft from the propeller across
the cockpit to the rudder—watched it tumble downward like a
shot mallard, sending up a geyser of water from the oil-slicked
surface of the sea.

"Ben—are you all right?"

"Huh? Oh, sure." Ben sipped his hot chocolate. "I just don't
agree with the Navy brass. I think we need every able-bodied man
where the fighting is."

Angela could see that talk of the war made Ben restless. "How's Rachel? I never see her around anymore."

Ben's mind leaped back to the present. "Fine. She spends a lot of time making baby clothes."

"Oh, that's wonderful! I didn't know," Angela declared, happy for the two of them. "When's the baby due?"

"April."

Noticing the gentle light that had come to Ben's eyes when he spoke of his wife and unborn child, Angela suddenly felt a heavy sadness settle over her, as cold and icy as the sleet she had left outside. She desperately needed to be loved, and the love that Ben so obviously shared with Rachel seemed to her so pure, so full of tenderness, that it caused her to weep in spite of all she could do to stop it. She bowed her head, both hands covering her eyes as unrelenting tears rolled down her cheeks.

Ben reached across the table taking her hand in his. "Angela, what's wrong? Are you sick?"

Weeping silently, Angela stared at Ben's blurry image, shaking her head slowly.

Taking a handkerchief from his coat pocket, Ben brushed her tears away, speaking in a hushed tone. "There, there. It can't be as bad as all that."

Angela took the handkerchief and finished wiping her eyes, dabbing at the wet trails of makeup that stained her cheeks. She had confided in no one since the death of her husband, not even Lila, but she felt strangely safe talking with Ben. "I'm sorry, Ben. It's just that I'm so lonely."

Ben knew the answer to Angela's loneliness and the terrible sorrow that was apparent in her eyes. He prayed that she would listen to him with an open heart. "Jesus loves you, Angela."

She paused in cleaning the makeup from her face, holding the handkerchief in both hands. "What? What did you say?"

"I said, 'Jesus loves you.'"

The sound of the name caused something to stir within the wounded heart of Angela Spain.

"Jesus is the answer to all your trouble," Ben continued, his voice strengthened by the conviction of his spirit. "I can't explain it. All I can do is to give you the message and tell you what he's done for me."

Angela sat perfectly still, her eyes full of wonder. She never expected something like this from Ben Logan.

"It was on the fantail of a ship in Sydney harbor when I first believed that Jesus is who he said he was." Ben stared past Angela and beyond the glare of the neon lit drugstore. "I was the most miserable man in the world. The girl I loved—or thought I loved—had dropped me flat, I got run out of my hometown, and I was just back to duty after my little brother's funeral."

"Pastor Shaw, Rachel's daddy, preached something at Pete's graveside service from the Book of John. Well, I started reading in the third chapter where the pastor's text had come from and by the time I got to chapter fifteen I had accepted Jesus as my Savior and Lord."

Angela glanced at Ben, then lowered her head. "But—but you don't know all the—things I've done."

"That's right. I don't." Ben touched her on the hand and she looked up into his eyes. "But Jesus does—and he loves you more than you could ever know. Nothing you could ever do would make him stop loving you."

"You think so?"

"I know so," Ben smiled and his face seemed to shine with the knowledge of what he said. He had never grown tired of telling the story of what Jesus had done for him; he found that the thrill and joy of it never diminished. "I know because he's my friend, and I can't explain that either, but he is. In the Book of John he told his disciples, 'I have called you friends.' And he'll be your friend, too, Angela, if you just let him."

Angela felt a struggle going on inside her. She wanted to get up and run from the drugstore, get in her car and drive forever out into the night. Gripping the table with all her might, she forced herself to speak. "I want Jesus. I want him to help me and take away this awful pain and loneliness. Could he do that for me, Ben? Could he?"

Ben squeezed her hand. "Oh, yes, Angela! That and so much more."

"But I don't know anything about religion."

"Doesn't matter. All you have to know is what God's word says and believe it."

"But there's no preacher."

"No, but Jesus is here. He said that he would never leave us or forsake us and that the Kingdom of God is within *you*." Ben took a small black New Testament from his jacket pocket. Without opening it he gazed directly into Angela's eyes and said, "'For God so loved the world, that he gave his only begotten Son, that whosoever believeth in him should not perish, but have everlasting life.'"

Ben had seen people come to Jesus before, and he knew that it was always accomplished by the power of the gospel, not by persuasive argument. He thumbed through a few pages of his New Testament until he came to the Book of Romans.

Angela could see that the pages of Ben's Bible had been marked and lined and dog-eared.

With no further preliminaries, Ben began to read in a clear tone, "'If thou shalt confess with thy mouth the Lord Jesus, and shalt believe in thine heart that God hath raised him from the dead, thou shalt be saved.'"

Looking up, Ben continued in his steady voice, "There's nothing we can do to earn salvation, Angela. Jesus did it all for us on the cross. Paul said, 'By grace are ye saved through faith . . . not of works, lest any man should boast.' It's a gift from God. All you have to do is accept it."

"But what do I do?"

"Just ask Jesus to save you."

Angela tried desperately to remember what she had learned about the Bible as a small child in Sunday school, but when she spoke, the prayer came directly from her heart. Closing her eyes, she bowed her head, still clinging to Ben's hand. "Jesus, I believe that you're God's son and that you died on the cross for me. I know I don't deserve it, but I ask you now to forgive me for all the wrong things I've done and make me the person that you would have me be."

Pausing, Angela glanced up at Ben, then lowered her head again. "I haven't read the Bible in years, and I don't know much about you, but if you'll just help me, Jesus, I'll live for you the rest of my life."

Ben found himself wiping tears from his eyes with the back of his hand. "Welcome to the family of God, Angela."

"I don't think I feel any different." Angela didn't know what to expect. She thought there might be some wondrous revelation from above, that the heavens would open or choirs of angels would sing some glorious song.

"That's all right. The Bible never says you have to *feel* a certain way to be a Christian. It's by faith, not feelings." Ben squeezed her hand again. "There's something I'm absolutely certain of though."

Angela stared at him wide-eyed, unaware of the tears that were spilling down her cheeks. "What's that?"

"The angels in heaven are rejoicing right now because you came to Jesus."

"How do you know that?" Angela gazed raptly into Ben's eyes as though he might be an Old Testament prophet come back to earth.

"Because God's word says it—that's how." Ben's face seemed to almost radiate light from the joy he felt. "Can you just imagine that? The angels of God up there singing and shouting praises because of what you just did. Can't you just hear them shouting, 'Glory to God, Angela's going to make heaven her home! Hallelujah, she came to Jesus!'"

Angela sat there smiling at Ben. She felt like she had never felt before although she didn't realize it then because she was so caught up in Ben's rejoicing for her. "I don't want to do anything wrong now, Ben, but I don't know what to do next."

Ben came back to himself, taking a deep breath before he spoke. "Excuse me. Sometimes I get a little carried away. Well, to start with you're going to make mistakes as long as you're in this world, Angela, so don't expect to be perfect. There *are* two things you need to do to start with though."

"What?" Angela was eager to do everything right.

"Take this and read it until you get your own Bible. I think the Book of John would be a good place to start." Holding out his New Testament toward her, Ben continued, "It's *so* important to stay in the Word, Angela. And remember no matter what *anyone* tells you, I don't care who it is—preacher, priest, the best person you know—if it contradicts this book, don't believe it."

Angela took the little Testament, holding it close to her breast. "What else?"

"Find yourself a good church."

"Where do I go?"

"Well, I think Rock Hill's a good church. That's where Rachel's daddy pastors," Ben said with some hesitation, not wanting to keep

Angela from finding her own way. "But God may have another place for you. Pray about it."

"I'm not sure I know how."

"Sure you do. You prayed a beautiful prayer tonight when you accepted Jesus. Start off by asking God to give you a good church to go to."

"All ready, Ben." Ollie stood behind the counter holding a white paper bag out toward the booth.

Ben stood up, taking Angela's hand to help her out of the booth. "Thanks, Mr. Caston. I know Mama really appreciates this. She hated to mess up your Christmas."

Ollie shook his head. "It's nothing. If it wasn't for folks like her, I couldn't afford that big turkey I got at home. Tell her and your whole family Merry Christmas for me."

Angela set both cups on the counter. "Thanks for the hot chocolate, Mr. Caston."

"You're quite welcome, Angela. Anything else I can do for you tonight?"

"No thanks. I'll be getting on home now. Merry Christmas to you."

"Same to you," Ollie smiled. "Watch yourself on the way home. It's getting nasty out there."

*   *   *

"Can I give you a ride home?" Angela walked along the sidewalk next to Ben.

"No thanks." Ben pointed down the street. "I'm in Daddy's log truck. Sure hope I don't have to drive Rachel to the hospital in that thing."

They stopped a half-block from Ollie's, standing beneath a streetlamp next to Angela's car. The sleet ticked rhythmically on the windshield and lay on the black surface of the car like beads of glass, glimmering in the pale light.

Ben gazed down at Angela's upturned face. It looked so much softer, almost like that of a child, as though years had fallen away in the last few minutes. "I'm so happy for you, Angela. I can't wait to tell my family."

Tears glistened in Angela's eyes. "Thank you, Ben. I owe you so much."

Laughing softly with the joy that seemed to overflow in him for Angela's new life, Ben shook his head slowly. "You don't owe me anything. It's just the way we Christians use the love that God pours out on his children. We give it away to others, and it just gets bigger and bigger."

Ben embraced Angela tenderly, and she pressed her soft cheek against his face. Beyond words now, Angela gave Ben a final smile and wiped the new tears from her eyes as she got into her car and drove toward home.

* * *

On the way, Angela heard the sound of the sleet on her car diminish, then stop completely. Snow began to fall; tiny flakes at first, and then larger, falling thick and heavy and soft through the beams of her headlights. She had never seen snow like this before. It was a dreamlike world she drove through now as though Liberty, Georgia, had been lifted up and set back down somewhere in Vermont.

Several times, feeling a presence in the car, she glanced at the passenger seat, but no one was there. It was a pleasant sensation, this snowfall dream of Liberty through the windshield and the comfort of an unseen Someone with her in the car.

Pulling underneath the portico, Angela turned off the headlights and sat for a few minutes watching the snowflakes drift and swirl in a silent soft whiteness across the flagstone patio and the lawn that receded into the darkness beyond the reach of the overhead light.

Angela got out of her car and ran up the concrete stairs with a lightness to her step she hadn't known since she chased fireflies in the star-spangled summer evenings of her childhood.

Taking the New Testament Ben had given her out of her pocket, she hung her jacket on the clothes tree and went into the kitchen. After making a pot of tea, she took Ben's gift over to the table, sat down and opened it to the Book of John.

"'In the beginning was the Word, and the Word was with God,

and the Word was God,'" she read out loud. "No wonder Ben thought it was so important to check out anything people tell me with what the Bible says."

Sipping her tea, Angela continued to read, and when something struck her as particularly important she would read it out loud, sometimes more than once.

"'And the light shineth in darkness; and the darkness comprehended it not.'" Angela pondered on this, thinking of the times she had sat in church not having the faintest idea what the pastor was talking about.

"'He was in the world, and the world was made by him, and the world knew him not.' Now isn't that something? Jesus made the world, and the world doesn't even know him. What a mixed-up bunch we human beings are."

Angela read the twelfth and thirteenth verses out loud and the words, underlined in Ben's book, seemed to ring through her soul like sweet music. "'But as many as received him, to them gave he power to become the sons of God, even to them that believe on his name: which were born, not of blood, nor of the will of the flesh, nor of the will of man, but of God.'"

"Oh, my Jesus! My Jesus. I truly believe in you. You seem like such a good friend already."

Angela read until she could no longer keep her eyes open. Then she showered, put on a freshly washed flannel nightgown, and took her little Testament to bed with her. After praying, it occurred to her that she had forgotten to be afraid and lonely in the vast and empty darkness of the house. In less than a minute she fell into a deep sleep, untroubled by the dreams that had tormented her.

* * *

Christmas morning dawned clear and cold with sunshine sparkling on the new-fallen snow. Angela dressed hurriedly in jeans and a white pullover sweater and rushed upstairs to the attic where she found a Nativity set and a hand-painted ceramic Christmas tree. Then she ran back downstairs into the spacious kitchen and set them up on one end of the long table.

"There, that looks all right, " she said, admiring her handiwork. "I guess it's kind of silly putting my Christmas decorations in the kitchen, but there's no tree in the living room anyway and these little things would be lost in that big room."

Angela made a pot of coffee and sat at the table drinking it from a bone-china cup while she stared wistfully at the manger with the tiny baby in it. "What a way to come into this world—in a dirty old stable. Well, I guess I might as well get used to it from the beginning. I'll never be able to understand why God does things the way he does."

Drinking the last of her coffee, Angela poured herself another cup and walked to the opposite end of the table. She leaned closer to the tiny child in the manger, staring at him and at his mother and father, wondering what must have gone through their minds to be part of God's eternal and wondrous gift to mankind. Suddenly her eyes grew bright with realization. "Today's his *birthday*. Happy birthday, Jesus!"

Angela hurried to the big walk-in pantry off the kitchen, returning with flour, baking soda, a bottle of vanilla extract, and a large can of Hershey's cocoa. Adding eggs and butter from the refrigerator as well as sugar from the canister that sat on the counter, she began blending it all together. Soon the warm, appetizing aroma of a cake baking began to fill the kitchen.

Unable to find any birthday candles, Angela returned to the attic where she located a foot-long red candle in a holder from last year's decorations. *Well, I guess this is better than nothing. Nobody'll see it but me anyway.*

Back in the kitchen, she mixed the chocolate icing in a bowl. When she took the cake out of the oven, she immediately began spreading the icing on it before it cooled. Pieces of cake began breaking off, falling to the table or sticking to her knife as she did her best to spread the icing evenly.

Standing back from the table, Angela observed her handiwork. "Well, let's hope it tastes better than it looks."

A sudden rapping on her back door, sounding almost as loud as gunfire in the stillness of the house, startled Angela. She looked down the hall through the dim foyer and saw Hartley Lambert's big blond face framed in the half-glass of the door.

Hartley, along with a few other pillars of the Liberty community, had begun to come skulking around Angela's back door at odd hours, starting a few days after her husband's funeral. She had always ignored them, refusing to even acknowledge that they were there.

Today she walked briskly across the foyer and jerked the door open. "Why, Mr. Lambert, whatever are you doing out here on Christmas morning?"

Bearlike in his heavy wool coat, Lambert's hard blue eyes lit up at the possibility of actually getting inside the house. "Just wanted to wish you a Merry Christmas, Angela. And I sure wish you'd call me Hartley."

Angela leaned to the side, looking behind him. "Where's Ellie and Debbie? I think a man should celebrate Christmas with his family. Don't you?"

Lambert gave her a sheepish grin. "Debbie's off somewhere and, well, you know how Ellie sometimes has a little too much—Christmas cheer. She probably won't get up till noon at least. Everybody's coming to the house at three o'clock for our annual get-together."

Gazing beyond Lambert, Angela found herself fascinated by the glittering whiteness of the morning. The world was covered with a soft blanket of snow, and the dark, leafless limbs of the trees shone with ice. The evergreens stood in bright fluffy rows. She felt that all this was another gift she had been given.

Lambert shivered, rubbing his hands together.

"Oh, I'm sorry! Come in, won't you?"

Lambert, grinning like a possum, followed Angela down the hall to the kitchen. *I knew she'd get lonesome for a man's company sooner or later, and ol' Hartley's got just the cure for a young widow left alone in this cruel world.*

"Coffee?"

"Yes, ma'am." Lambert sat down at the table without being asked.

Angela poured the coffee and sat it in front of him. He managed to brush against her hand as he reached for the sugar and spooned some into his coffee.

As Lambert sipped his drink, his eyes roamed the kitchen, falling on the opposite end of the table. "Funny place for Christmas decorations, ain't it?

"I don't think so," Angela smiled back brightly.

"Hm." Lambert noticed the cake on the counter. "That thing looks like somebody frosted it with a claw hammer. What's the cake for?"

"It's a birthday cake."

"Yours?"

"No." Angela picked up the cake, placing it on the table next to Lambert. "Want some?"

Lambert looked as though she had offered him a plate of worms. "No thanks. I'm not very hungry. Why did you use such a big candle?"

"It's all I could find."

Never saw a candle like that on a cake before. Lambert's curiosity finally got the best of him. "Whose birthday is it anyway?"

"Why, Mr. Lambert, you mean you don't know?"

"Hartley, please! Call me Hartley. You make me feel like an old man." He began to shift about in his chair. This was not at all what he had expected. "No I don't know whose birthday it is."

"Jesus."

"Jesus?" Hartley glanced over his shoulder as though looking for the nearest exit. "What about him?"

"It's his birthday."

"But he's . . ."

"He's here with *me*, Mr. Lambert," Angela replied sweetly, feeling almost ashamed at what she was doing. "He said that he'd never leave me or forsake me."

Nutty women—why do I always have to get hooked up with nutty women? It's not enough that I've got to live with one. "That's nice." Lambert took a last swallow of coffee and pushed his chair back from the table.

"You sure you don't want a piece of cake? I think it tastes better than it looks."

Lambert glanced over at the ragged cake. A piece of the chocolate icing oozed down the side, dropping off on the plate. "No— really. I need to lose a few pounds."

"Can't blame you, I guess. It does look kind of like I left it out in a thunderstorm."

"Well, thanks for the coffee." Lambert got out of his chair, walking quickly out of the kitchen.

Angela followed him down the hall to the back door. As he stepped out onto the landing at the top of the stairs, she called to him, "Mr. Lambert."

He twisted his head around as he held on to the rail on his way down. "What?"

"I just wanted to wish you a Merry Christmas. Be sure to give Ellie my best."

Lambert grunted as he reached the back drive, then he got into his big black Packard and gunned the engine. As he drove away, Angela saw him talking to himself.

Part 3

THE SIDEWALKS OF LIBERTY

9

HOME

J.T. Dickerson had been sober for a solid month. Having grown weary of his erratic behavior and hours, Lila had told him that the next time he didn't show when he was supposed to he would be barred from the premises of the *Journal*.

"I'm proud of you, J.T." Lila shuffled through several sheets of copy she was proofing as she talked. Wearing a tan blouse and a brown gathered skirt with pockets at the hips, she looked the picture of businesslike efficiency.

Wondering why he found the *Journal* and its sometimes fractious owner so attractive, J.T. felt like a sixteen-year-old on his first date although he had never broached the subject of actually going out with Lila. "Don't get carried away with yourself, editor. It's just a trial separation. The bottle and I shared a lot of years together."

Giving him a stern glance over her gold-rimmed reading glasses, Lila continued her work. "I'm not trying to rehabilitate you, J.T., and I'm through preaching."

"Well, that's certainly a relief." J.T. hopped up on a desktop across from Lila, letting his legs dangle loosely over the side. "I'm afraid it may be a little late though. I think you've quoted most of the Bible to me already."

Lila finished her work and shoved the stack of paper aside, noticing the sly smile on J.T.'s lean face. She thought he looked quite presentable in his ironed khakis and wine-colored Harvard sweatshirt. He had freshly shaved and his thick brown hair was combed, although it was shaggy around the ears and neck. "You truly have been a lifesaver, J.T. If you hadn't gotten places like Hightower's and Three Corners' Grocery to handle the *Journal* we probably would have gone out of business. People pick up a lot of papers in those stores."

J.T. waved Lila's gratitude away with a flick of his hand. "You're not doing bad for a weekly tabloid, but I've been studying on this situation some. I've got some ideas that could help the *Journal* become a strong daily."

Lila knew J.T. was pausing for effect. She got up from her swivel chair, walked over to the coffee service, and poured a cup, holding it out in his direction.

Shaking his head, J.T. continued as Lila took her seat. "You know what you're doing wrong?"

"I know," Lila sighed. "I'm only a helpless little woman in a man's world and that just isn't done down here in the 'Land of Cotton.'"

"Wrong, Mrs. William Randolph Hearst," J.T. replied calmly. "You think because you spent a few years up in Chicago, you got all the answers."

Lila, playing an imaginary banjo, hummed the last few notes of "Dixie." Finishing with a flourish, she sang, "Look away, Dixieland."

J.T. gave her a smattering of applause. "Now if you're finished with your minstrel show, let's get down to business."

"Sorry. I think these months back in the South may have loosened me up a tad too much. Or maybe I'm having trouble believing that you're not putting me on. You've been known to do that before."

"I guess I deserve the doubts, but this time I'm serious. You're trying to compete with Dobe Jackson on his own ground and you can't win." J.T. hopped off the desk and began pacing back and forth. "It's like strapping claws on your fingers to go bear hunting. The bear would always win."

"Elucidate." Lila leaned back in her chair, holding her cup in both hands. "I'm afraid your parables are a little more complex than the ones I'm used to."

J.T. stopped, stared at Lila with mock ferocity, and resumed his pacing. "Well, Dobe's got the latest teletype and every other advantage that money can buy. He runs all the top syndicated columnists, gets the war news first. He's got all the technical advantages. You've got to simplify."

"And just where do I begin?"

"Picture journalism."

"How do you know about the newspaper business?" Lila was becoming intrigued with J.T.'s monologue now that she saw he meant business.

"I have a library card," J.T. smirked, reaching for his wallet. "Want to see it?"

"I'll take your word for it."

J.T. sat back down on the desk. The morning light streaming in the windows behind him threw his face into shadow, forming a border of diffused light around it. "More pictures. Preferably of Liberty and places close by. The folks around here would just eat it up."

Lila stared thoughtfully at the bright windows. "I think you're on to something. All I've been giving them is the boring facts about people they'll never see."

"Yep. And I'm not through yet." J.T. ran his fingers through his thick brown hair, brushing it back from his eyes. "A profile every week on one of our local boys in the armed forces. Not just hit or miss, but until the war's over. Talk to his family, teachers, friends—anybody that's close to him. Call the column something patriotic like," J.T. made a flourish with his hand as he created each title, "'Proudly They Serve' or 'Our Boys in Uniform'—even better, 'Liberty Goes to War.'"

Lila was out of her chair now, taking over for J.T. by pacing back and forth excitedly. "By george, I think you've done it, J.T. It's just the kind of thing that's so simple no one in the business has thought of it. Obviously Dobe Jackson and that bunch over at the *Herald* haven't."

"There's more."

Lila stopped, rubbing the back of her neck with her left hand as she gazed at J.T. "More?"

"I've even got your first story for you." J.T. felt good about being able to help Lila out, especially since the odds were stacked against her. He considered the waste in his life and thought maybe he was trying to make up for some of it.

"Pray do go on, Mr. Dickerson," Lila smiled with mock formality. "You're really on a roll."

"Clay McCain."

"With so many boys overseas, why choose him?"

"Because you can get pictures and a personal interview. He's coming home Friday."

"But he's only been gone . . ." Lila thought back to that day the previous October when she and Angela had seen Clay bidding his farewells to his family and Diane Jackson, "six months. Why's he coming home so soon?"

"He got wounded in the fighting at Tarawa." J.T. remembered Clay as a rambunctious little boy and thought of the times they had played ball together in the little courtyard behind his office. "From what I hear it was one of the bloodiest battles of the war. The Marines won't forget about Tarawa for a long time."

Lila thought about what a fine strapping young man she had seen on the station platform that October morning when Clay had left for the Marines. Shaking her head sadly, she spoke in a somber voice. "It's so sad! All these fine young men losing their lives or coming home with terrible wounds."

J.T. remembered his war, "The Great War—The War to End All Wars." He could almost hear the screams of men having legs amputated when the anesthesia was gone; could almost see the pale fear-ravaged faces of his men as they went "over the top," charging headlong across the cratered, blackened landscape of France into the hail of machine-gun bullets and shrapnel. "It's more than *sad*. There's *no* word for what it is."

Lila had known for some time that J.T. had fought in World War I, but he had never spoken of it. She decided to press ahead with the subject at hand. "Loads of pictures and news that's close to the hearts of the people. I think you've found the formula for the *Journal's* success, J.T."

The lines in J.T.'s forehead slowly faded. "Yep. Don't forget me when you make your first million."

"What do you mean forget you?" Lila smiled. "You're going to be right here to help me make it—aren't you?"

"I don't think I follow you."

Lila went back behind her desk and sat down. "You mean to tell me you're going to come in here, drop this marvelous idea on me— and then just walk out the door? Why that's absolutely ludicrous."

"I've been known to be ludicrous in my time. In fact I've all but elevated it to an art form." J.T. shrugged. "But I usually know why."

"Because I've got no way to put your ideas into motion without you."

J.T. had a feeling he was going to regret his enthusiastic re-search into the newspaper business. "I'm not a newspaper man, Lila."

"Maybe not, but in about two days I can sure remedy that." Lila felt sure she had him trapped. "As a lawyer you already know how to investigate—gather pertinent information and organize it into a comprehensive written document."

"But . . ."

"Just give me two minutes," Lila interrupted. "All you have to do is forget the legal mumbo jumbo and write it in everyday language."

"Are you kidding?" J.T. gave her an incredulous stare. "I'm a lawyer. The whole legal profession is based on making things as obscure as possible."

Lila put her hands on her hips, tilting her head slightly to the side. "I'm trying to be serious here, J.T. This could be a whole new career for you."

"You think I'm kidding about this? You ever hear a lawyer make any sense when he's talking about anything to do with his work?"

Her brow knitted in thought, Lila replied slowly, "Hm—I guess I haven't."

"That's why we make such good politicians. Nobody ever has the slightest idea what we're talking about," J.T. continued, "and you can never get a straight answer to any question—unless maybe you're asking for the correct time."

Lila turned a level stare on J.T. "You gonna help me out or not?"

J.T. felt like something was caught in his throat when he tried to speak.

Seeing an opening, Lila rushed ahead. "You know *everybody* in town. All you have to do is stick to the bedrock of journalism—Who? What? Where? Why? When? and How?—and Presto! You're my star reporter."

"I think all those Chicago winters froze a good part of your brain cells, Lila." It had been a long time since J.T. had taken on a job where he would have to show up every week, and the proximity to this one had already begun to give him the willies. "You'll have to do it yourself."

"Can't."

"What do you mean—*can't?* It's your newspaper. You can do what you want to."

"First of all I don't have the time to take on anything new. I'm doing a half-dozen jobs already. Second, you know as well as I do that this little project would be perfect for you. I'm still just a Yankee outsider."

"You're a hard woman to say no to, Lila." J.T. turned, putting his hand on the doorknob. "I'll give it a try. But I dictate the column—somebody else is doing the typing."

"Deal." Lila walked over to the door and shook J.T.'s hand before he could leave.

J.T. cleared his throat. "I should have had better sense than to cut your grass when you first got here. One little favor and suddenly I'm your indentured servant."

Lila laughed softly. "Oh, it's not that bad! You'll love it—just wait and see."

J.T. grunted and stepped through the door.

*   *   *

The American offensive in the fall of 1943 called for a strike at the biggest of the Gilbert Islands on the morning of November 20. No one expected any tough resistance from the Japanese. Tarawa had been bombed for a full week and was pounded by the huge fourteen-inch guns from battleships for hours before the attack took place. In spite of this, almost all the 4,500 Japanese, sheltered inside their sand-covered concrete bunkers, survived.

Admiral Kelly Turner had been warned about the tricky waters around the island as there was a chance that the tides would be low then. He decided to take the risk—and lost.

The first waves of Marines assaulted the beaches in amphibious tractors called Amtracks. They made it. But the next waves in the flat-bottomed Higgins boats began crashing onto the coral reefs that were covered by only three feet of water. With the boats unable to cross the reefs, the Marines had to wade hundreds of yards to the beaches under murderous fire from the Japanese. Only about half of them made it.

Admiral Keiji Shibasaki, the Japanese commander had

boasted, "A million men cannot take Tarawa in a hundred years." He was wrong. Fifty-six hundred Marines took it in three days, but at a terrible cost: 991 dead, 2,311 wounded; 17 Japanese survived.

On the morning of November 20, 1943, Clayton McCain was a strong, confident nineteen-year-old hardened combat veteran with three campaigns to his credit. At sunrise on November 23, after surviving the last desperate banzai attack, he looked as though he had aged twenty years when two stretcher-bearers carried him, filthy, smoke-blackened, and hollow-eyed, down to the beach.

* * *

By the spring of 1944, the high school band no longer welcomed the sons of Liberty home on the station platform when they returned wounded or on leave. No crowds gathered waving flags and singing "God Bless America" for their returning heroes. Too many coffins had been unloaded and wheeled across to the depot since that Sunday morning attack on Pearl Harbor. Too many sons and husbands and brothers now lay beneath the shadow of the tilting old tombstones in the cemeteries of Liberty.

The railway station was still an exciting place for children and the dwindling few who were as yet exempt from personal tragedy as a result of the war. But for the majority of Liberty's citizens, the homecoming celebrations had worn thin. The bright and gaudy decorations and the patriotic songs had been undermined by the lingering memories of flower-scented funeral parlors and the sound of muffled weeping.

* * *

Clay couldn't imagine that he had actually lived in the town he viewed through the window as the train began slowing down to pull into the station at Liberty. From the height of the trestle, he gazed down on the green and shimmering water of the river where he had gone swimming and fishing; he saw the knotted rope hanging from the same lofty oak limb where he and his childhood friends had swung out from the bank high over the swimming hole and plunged with a stomach-churning dive into the water.

He viewed the high school and the baseball diamond in the

shimmering distance and watched his neighbors working in their April-bright flowerbeds or walking along shady sidewalks beneath the ancient elms and oaks and cedars. Downtown, people shopped and visited and did all the dozens of other things that made up their safe and comfortable days as though death had no road map to Liberty, Georgia.

Clay knew that this was his hometown, the place where he was born and raised; he knew that these all-too-familiar people were his own family and friends and neighbors. But he knew it in the same way a man knows he has a fatal wound—with knowledge and pain, but with no true acceptance of the reality of it, as though he could never be touched by the immutable hand of mortality.

The train stopped alongside the station platform with a hissing of steam and the successive jolting of the railroad cars. Clay sat perfectly still behind the protective glass. He felt that if he could carry the window off the train with him, he would be protected from whatever awaited him in this familiar and foreign place where the Marines had sent him at last.

He longed for a friend and knew that none awaited him on the other side of the glass, knew that they had all disappeared in blossoms of fire and thunder when shells had found their Amtracks or Higgins boats, or died screaming as they clutched the cold Japanese steel in their bellies, or simply dropped without a sound plunging through the surf toward the beach. No one in this strange and clean and vexingly quiet place that lay beyond the window could ever replace them.

Still, he longed desperately for a friend.

*　*　*

"Clay, I didn't think you were due home until tomorrow." J.T. walked briskly across the depot waiting room toward Clay who sat at a table gazing through one of the tall windows that looked out onto the station platform. His Marine uniform, complete with red chevrons on the shoulders and three rows of campaign ribbons across the left side of his chest, hung loosely on his tall frame. The toes of his side-buckled combat boots gleamed like mirrors in the slanting sunlight.

Clay had deliberately taken an earlier train so no one would be at the station to greet him. He was grateful though that if someone had to find him this soon after his arrival, it was J.T. instead of Diane or his parents.

With some misgivings Clay tried to sound happy to see him. "Hey there, J.T. Who taught you how to shave?" The words sounded as though they had been spoken by someone he used to know a long time ago.

"Well, when I finally hit puberty, I just had to learn," J.T. shot back. Then with a sheepish grin he continued. "Actually it kinda goes with the job."

"Ironed khakis and a clean shirt. You look pretty good cleaned up. Sit down and I'll buy you a cup of coffee." Clay heard himself speaking as normally as he always had with J.T., but he still felt like an impostor.

"Sure thing, but I'll go get it." J.T. walked across the polished plank floor and dropped two dimes on the counter, returning with two thick white mugs of coffee. As he came up behind Clay to set his coffee on the table, he surveyed him quickly from head to toe but could see no sign of a wound. He decided not to ask him about his injuries for now.

"I believe my hearing's going bad on me." Clay leaned his head to one side, tapping on his ear with the flat of his hand. "I thought I heard you say something about a job."

"Well, it's *almost* like a job," J.T. nodded, noticing how thin Clay was. It was as though the months he had spent in the Marine Corps had pared him down to bone and muscle. "Part-time reporter for Lila Kronen."

Clay's eyes narrowed in thought. "Lila Kronen . . . Oh, yeah. She's that Yankee from Chicago who was trying to start the *Journal* up again."

J.T. stared directly at Clay's eyes. They looked hollow and dull and seemed to be focused on something in midair halfway across the room. "She did start it up again. It's been a hard road, but the lady's got gumption."

"I expect Mr. Jackson was a big help to her, wasn't he? I know he must love the idea of another newspaper opening up in town," Clay remarked, thinking of Diane and how much he didn't want to have to face her—at least for a while.

J.T. grunted and sipped his coffee. "Dobe's had things his own sweet way for a lot of years. Maybe it's time somebody came along with some new ideas."

"New ideas? In Liberty?"

"That is asking a lot, isn't it?" J.T. smiled. "Maybe she'll just rework the old ones for the time being. Then go for a hot new issue like women's suffrage."

Clay caught J.T. watching him with a curious expression on his face. *What am I doing wrong? I wonder if I look all right.* He quickly picked up his mug and took a swallow of coffee to hide the self-conscious feeling.

J.T. noticed Clay's motion when he reached for the mug. He had leaned his right shoulder forward a bit to compensate for the arm that stayed slightly bent at the elbow. It kept that exact same angle as he sat the mug back down. He was afraid that he had embarrassed Clay and felt ashamed that he was holding him under a microscope. *I wonder if it's serious enough to end his baseball career?* "Want to hear something funny?"

"Yeah. I could use a laugh."

"It's about my job."

"That's pretty funny by itself—you and the word *job* spoken in the same breath." Clay tried to grin, feeling that his mouth had forgotten how. "Far back as I can remember, you took just enough cases in your law practice to keep from having to live in a cardboard box in the alley behind Ollie's Drugstore."

"Me with a job. I guess it is kinda funny at that." J.T. glanced again at Clay's eyes, being careful not to make him uneasy. He remembered that same vacant stare in the eyes of men who had spent too many months in the muddy fields and trenches of the Ardennes and Belleau Wood.

Clay merely nodded as though the conversation was taxing his reserves.

J.T. tried to lighten the dialogue. "You still haven't asked what's unusual about my job. Your lack of interest makes me feel kinda like it may not have the profound consequences I expect it to for the future of our country."

Clay almost laughed. "Tell me quick, before I bust a gut trying to figure it out."

"It's you."

"Me?"

"Yeah. You're my first assignment."

Clay shrugged, waiting for an explanation.

"Stories for the *Journal* about our boys in the armed forces. Not just the MacArthur's and Patton's and Eisenhower's that Dobe runs in the *Herald*." J.T. rubbed his chin with his forefinger. "I guess it'll be kind of like Ernie Pyle's columns—you know, stories about the ordinary soldiers."

"Everybody likes Ernie's stuff."

"Well, there'll be some notable exceptions in my work," J.T. explained.

"Like what?"

"First of all the quality of the writing won't be the same—Ernie can't hope to compete with me," J.T. grinned. "And second I'm not about to go traipsing all over the world like he does. Seeing one war up close is enough."

Clay hunched his shoulders slightly and seemed to shrink inside himself. He could almost hear the pop of the mortar tubes and the heavy crunching sound as they hit, sending hot shrapnel whining overhead. Laying his left hand on the right, he rubbed it back and forth across his knuckles.

"You OK, son?"

Clay took a deep breath. "I don't think I'm in the mood to talk right now."

"Don't blame you," J.T. agreed quickly, remembering how little he had spoken of his own war in the past quarter of a century since he had returned from it.

Realizing he was slumping in his chair, Clay sat up straight, but continued to rub his knuckles.

"Guess you'll take it easy for a while, huh?"

"I guess so."

"Maybe do a little fishing."

"Maybe."

J.T. hated to leave Clay alone; he wished he had the words to make things easier for him but could see that he had tolerated about all the company he could for the time being. "Guess I'd better get moving. Got to pick up a package for the *Journal*."

Clay tried to smile, but again his lips felt unable to fit themselves around one. "Good seeing you, J.T."

"You too, Clay." J.T. stood up and shoved his chair under the table. "See you again soon."

"You bet."

10

SHADOWS

"Aren't you having a good time, Clay?" Diane Jackson had worn her best party dress for the occasion. Cornflower blue with thin straps and a full skirt, it was designed to show her figure to its best advantage. "After all, Mother and I went to a lot of trouble to plan this affair for your homecoming."

Seated next to Diane on a stone bench in a shadowed alcove of myrtle trees, Clay stared across the long expanse of lawn toward the lighted terrace of the Jackson home. At Diane's insistence, he had worn his Marine dress uniform complete with campaign ribbons and his Silver Star. He hated wearing it now that he had been discharged from the Corps, but she had said that she wanted to show off her hero to everybody.

Couples danced to "I'll Walk Alone," played by a tuxedoed band of locals in a yellow gazebo. White-jacketed Negro waiters with trays laden with champagne walked among the elegantly dressed guests. A huge "Welcome Home Clay" banner hung from the eaves of the house. "I appreciate all the work you and your mother did, Diane. I guess I'm just not very good company right now."

Diane had been listening to the same excuse for two weeks and was running out of patience. "Well, you'll just have to *make* yourself good company then."

Clay, his elbows resting on his knees, glanced sideways at her without speaking.

Taking his hand, Diane spoke in a softer tone. "You're going to have to pull yourself out of this, Clay. All you have to do is be like you used to be."

"Is that all?" Clay stood up, pulling his hand free of Diane's. "Why didn't I think of that?"

"Won't you even try?" Diane rose and took his arm just above the elbow.

Clay flinched, drawing his arm away, his lips drawn thin from the pain.

"Oh, I'm so sorry! I forgot." Diane clasped her hands at her breast.

"Forget it."

Taking his hand gently, Diane guided him back to the bench. "Clay . . ."

Clay stared between his knees.

"You've just got to try and help yourself. For my sake," Diane pleaded. "And your mother's worried to death about you. You come and go at all hours, sleep all day, and ramble around who knows where all night . . ."

Clay tried to shut out the noise of Diane's rambling speech, finding it a bothersome and unnecessary drone in the forefront of the party noise.

" . . . even thought about going to work and . . ."

Clay found himself inexplicably drifting toward rage. Diane's voice somehow became entangled in his mind with the high-pitched taunts of the Japanese soldiers from the shell-blasted darkness of Tarawa. Just prior to a banzai charge, they had screamed the atrocities that they would commit on the Americans.

" . . . and even Daddy said that . . ."

Squeezing his hands together, Clay shut his eyes tightly as though it would block out the sound.

"Clay, what's wrong?"

Clay turned to Diane and saw her face grow suddenly pale as he looked at her. Her eyes widened and her mouth formed an O with an intake of breath.

Shaking his head, Clay fought off the anger and fear that had driven him for months in the Pacific. He reached out and took Diane's hand. "It's OK now. Really. I'm all right."

Diane relaxed, squeezing his hand. "Clay, you had the strangest look in your eyes. Almost like you . . ." she looked away " . . . wanted to hurt me."

"Don't even think such a thing!" Clay could see the fear in her eyes and feel the trembling of her hand. He knew he had to make things better quickly before she had time to think about the glimpse she had had inside him.

"I almost felt . . . afraid of you."

From the gazebo near the house, the band began to play "Rum and Coca-Cola."

Forcing a lightness to his voice, Clay pulled her up from the bench. "C'mon. Let's cut a rug.

Diane's voice cracked slightly as she answered. "That's all right. We don't have to."

"No. C'mon. I really want to."

Diane smiled, stepped around him, and took his left arm as they walked across the damp grass.

*　*　*

"Whew! That last one just about did me in." Sipping a glass of champagne, Clay leaned against the stone railing that bordered the terrace.

Diane stood next to him, gazing up into his face with an expression of adoration mixed with wonder at the abrupt change that had come over him. "I'm so glad you're having a good time. I thought you might have forgotten how."

Clay grinned the way he had before he left for the South Pacific. "How could I not have a good time with the prettiest girl in Georgia next to me?"

"Oh, Clay, I'm so glad you're happy!" Diane leaned against him, circling his lean waist with her arms. She lifted herself up on tiptoe to kiss him on the cheek.

"Want some more champagne?" Clay held his empty glass out in front of him.

"No thanks," Diane smiled sleepily. "I'm kind of lightheaded already."

"Be right back."

Clay walked across the flagstone terrace toward a bar set up outside the French doors that led to the dining room. Decorated with red, white, and blue bunting, it was manned by a Negro with skin so dark it had an almost purple hue to it in the light from inside the house. His starched white jacket looked as stiff as cardboard on his bony frame.

"Hey, I 'member you. Cletus Felder, right?" Clay greeted him with a big smile, clapping him on the shoulder. "We worked together at the lumbermill one summer."

Hearing Clay's too-loud greeting, Dobe Jackson glanced over his shoulder, frowning at the familiarity that Clay was sharing with his bartender.

"Yas, suh. Sho' did." Felder replied. "I still works there. Mr. Dobe he let me bartend sometimes to make a little extra change. I got nine head of young'uns."

"Doggone it's good to see you." Clay felt more at ease than he had since his return to Liberty. "Ol' Hartley's a tough man to work for, ain't he?"

Felder glanced around him. "No suh. Hit ain't so bad when you gets used to it."

"Ain't so bad! Who you kidding?" With his champagne-muddled thinking, Clay hadn't noticed that he was making Felder extremely uncomfortable. "We used to talk so bad about him I bet his ears were burning."

"Kin I git you something, suh?"

"Oh, yeah." Clay glanced at the assortment of bottles lining the shelf behind Felder. "I think I'll have a taste of that sour mash over there with a Coke on the side."

"Yes, suh."

Clay watched Felder pour three fingers of amber liquid into a shot glass, open a bottle of Coke from a galvanized tub of ice, and set it down next to the bourbon. Turning the shot glass up, he emptied it, shuddering as the fiery liquid burned down his throat. Grabbing the bottle of Coke, he gulped at it greedily until it was empty.

Felder watched in amazement, shaking his head slightly and making a small clucking sound under his breath.

"Whoa! That'll clear out your sinuses in a hurry," Clay gasped, slamming the bottle down on the bar.

"Could I speak with you a moment, Clay?" Dobe Jackson, wearing an elegantly tailored black tuxedo and ruffled white shirt, stood behind him. Jackson despised the thought of his daughter dating someone from a working-class background like Clay.

Considering it a personal affront to his standing in the community, he looked for every opportunity to chastise him about his lack of social graces.

Clay turned around, his eyes shining from the alcohol. "Why, certainly."

Jackson motioned for Clay to follow him. He walked down the side steps of the terrace and over to a shadowed area near an inside corner of the house. "I don't think it's a good idea—this fraternizing with the hired help."

"The hired help," Clay frowned, his brain fuzzy from the rush of alcohol. "Oh, you mean Cletus! He's a real good fellow—hard worker."

"You miss my point."

Clay shrugged.

"Hard work isn't the issue here," Jackson explained with exasperation. "It gives our other guests a bad impression of you. If you're going to see my daughter, you must remember at all times that image is important. You can't go around acting like white trash in front of our friends and family."

Clay stared at the haughty, condescending expression on Jackson's fleshy face. He suddenly lost the false sense of tranquility that the liquor had given him and felt a familiar rage build inside his gut, rising through his chest and up into his temples. For reasons he no longer tried to fathom, nothing was funny anymore. A red glow seemed to spread across his field of vision as the warmth reached his face.

The change in Clay was not lost on Jackson. He saw the dull, somewhat foolish expression dissipate from Clay's face, saw the dark granite gleam come into his eyes. Taking an involuntary step backward, Jackson stumbled over an empty champagne bottle. Arms flailing in the air, he leaned against the side of the house, regaining his balance just before he fell down.

Clay's face smiled, but his eyes remained cold and remote as though untouched by what was happening around him. "Are you all right, sir?"

"What?" Jackson pushed away from the house, straightening his bow tie. "Oh, yes. I'm fine."

"You sure?"

"Quite. If you'll excuse me, I must see to our guests." Jackson turned, walking briskly away with a single quick glance over his shoulder.

Clay took a deep breath, walked up the low flight of steps to the terrace, and over to the bar. "I believe I'll have a little more of that whiskey, Cletus."

"Yas, suh." He reached for a shot glass, set it on the table, and grabbed the square, black-labeled bottle.

Clay shoved the glass aside with the back of his hand. "Don't need this, Cletus."

"Yas, suh."

Popping the cork, Clay turned the bottle up and took a long swallow. A slow smile spread over his face. "Mighty good for what ails you, Cletus."

Glancing around, Cletus spoke in a low tone. "You gonna git sick, Mr. Clay."

"I am sick, Cletus." He waved his hand at the crowd around him. "Sick of all this."

"Come on now, Mr. Clay," Cletus pleaded. "Don't act like that. Dis whole thing for you."

"You're a good man, Cletus." Clay clapped him on the shoulder. "Better'n any of us."

"Don't mess up," Cletus warned, walking down the bar to serve a lady with golden hair and a silver dress.

Clay gazed over at Diane who was talking with Keith Demerie. He wore a replica of Dobe Jackson's tuxedo and looked very much like a bigger, younger version of Diane's father. Catching Clay's eye, Diane waved at him. Clay nodded, waited until she turned back to Demerie, then tucked the bottle under his jacket and walked down the terrace steps and out into the darkness.

* * *

Clay loved the sidewalks of Liberty. Taking an occasional swallow from his bottle, he followed them past the white two-story houses with their high wraparound porches and slate roofs. Shaded by ancient oaks, they had the air of gentle and satisfied old ladies who had lived their lives well. The mild April air carried the scent of roses, jasmine, and wisteria from the flowerbeds on their well-tended lawns.

But the scent of the sweet olive trees brought a sharp pain to Clay's chest. It all came back to him in a headlong rush of memory: the golden sunlight pouring down on the baseball diamond, the sticky feel of the rosin bag in his hand, and the sound of his fastball slapping against the catcher's mitt as he fanned another batter, and the sight of Ted Williams sitting in the bleachers—the greatest hitter in the game come all the way from Boston to watch him throw his fastball. He remembered the warm pride that flowed through him—and the cold prospect of failure.

Only two years had passed and to Clay it seemed as though it had happened in another lifetime to someone else. He found it more and more difficult to live with the man he was now, this man who was only a few months old—born on a blackened and torn coral island in the South Pacific amid the thunder of artillery shells and the screams of the dying, born with an arm no better than anyone else's.

Clay sat down on a wide concrete banister at the bottom of some steps that led up to a sloping lawn. He drew the bittersweet fragrance of the sweet olive deeply into his lungs and along with it the pain of remembrance. Pulling the cork from the bottle, he lifted it to his mouth. Then he held it at arm's length and turned it upside down over the sidewalk, listening to it gurgle empty.

Staring at the spreading stain of whiskey on the sidewalk, Clay lost himself in images of the major leagues as he had done countless times on the cramped Liberty ships or in a sandy foxhole. He could almost hear the roar of the crowd from the tiers of the cavernous stadium as he walked onto the manicured grass of the freshly striped infield; he could almost see headlines the next morning announcing another victory.

From an open window the sound of the Inkspots singing "A Lovely Way to Spend an Evening" drifted on the scented air.

Clay laughed bitterly and spoke out loud. "This certainly is a lovely way to spend an evening."

"I agree."

Startled, Clay leaped to his feet. He saw his high school English teacher, Leslie Gifford, walking slowly toward him. "Oh, hello, Mr. Gifford."

Crippled from polio, Gifford walked with a loosely swinging left arm and a right foot that slapped softly against the rough concrete sidewalk. He wore a tweed jacket from long habit, even though the evening was mild. He hardly realized anymore that it was to make his disability less noticeable. "I didn't mean to sneak up on you like that."

I must be losing my touch. No one would have gotten that close without me hearing them—not before . . . "Guess I was daydreaming." Clay glanced around him as though he just realized where he was. "Can you daydream at night? I never thought about that before."

"I suppose so," Gifford quipped, easing the weight of his stiletto-slim body onto his left leg. The stance gave a barely noticeable "S" curve to his body. "As long as you don't go to sleep. Then it doesn't count."

Clay smiled, remembering Gifford's unusual sense of humor from the classroom.

"So—what's the local hero doing out here all by himself?" Gifford continued, brushing his light-brown hair back out of his eyes. Unfashionably long, it touched his ears as well as his shirt collar. His eyes, the color of old pecan shells, held a strange sad light as he spoke. "I didn't think the lovely Diane Jackson ever let you out of her sight."

"I think her daddy would just as soon she never laid eyes on me again."

"Somehow that doesn't surprise me."

"Why?" Clay was puzzled. He thought Gifford had always been fond of him, even to the point of helping him with special writing projects on the weekends. "Is there something wrong with me?"

"Most assuredly."

"What is it?"

"You have a deficiency that is patently obscene and virtually unforgivable in the mind of Dobe Jackson." Gifford spoke in a grave and level voice; the light from the street lamp cast a soft luminescent glow over his face. With his small nose, full lips, and softly rounded chin women found him attractive in spite of the ravages of polio.

Clay let Gifford ramble on, thinking the solitary life he had chosen to lead with only his books for company most of the time caused him to be a little strange and unpredictable.

"Aren't you going to ask me what it is?" Gifford thought Clay was losing interest in the game.

"I did."

"Impecuniousness."

"Impecu—that sounds like one of those South Pacific diseases. What in the world does it mean?"

"You ain't got no money," Gifford explained in his best Georgia twang. "That's what it means, and that's why ol' Dobe will never be your bosom buddy."

"I'm not exactly choked up that he isn't." Clay always enjoyed Gifford's company and felt better after talking with him for only a few minutes. He thought it might be because Gifford hadn't asked him what he planned to do with his life. "Why don't you sit down a minute?"

"Don't mind if I do." Gifford stepped over and leaned against the concrete banister across from Clay's. "I certainly don't have anything pressing at the moment."

"Mr. Gifford, if you don't mind my asking, why do you always do everything alone?" Clay would never have asked a question so personal of anyone before he went to the South Pacific for fear that he would insult them or be rebuked, but now that possibility didn't seem to matter one way or the other. He was beginning to learn that fears he had before he went into the corps were no longer a part of his makeup.

Gifford reflected on the question a few moments. "Never thought of it much—maybe because no one ever asked me before. I guess it's just my way."

"That girl's PE coach wasn't too happy about it being just your way if I remember right," Clay ventured, considering himself a man of the world and perfectly qualified to discuss women with an educated man like Gifford.

Gifford glanced at him with a wry smile. "You knew about that, did you?"

"I think the whole school knew," Clay replied, enjoying this welcome respite from eyes that he considered more accusing than caring.

"An innocent diversion."

Clay tapped the whiskey bottle gently between his knees. It clinked against the concrete banister, reminding him that Gifford had said nothing about his drinking. "More like a romance according to the school gossip."

"A couple of movies and a fountain Coke at Ollie's hardly qualifies as romance."

"What was her name? I must be getting old." Clay remembered the pretty blonde teacher who had spent only one year at Liberty High, ostensibly leaving (and it was the prime topic of conversation in the girls' bathroom for weeks) because of the pain of her unrequited love for Leslie Gifford.

"Tennerman," Gifford offered solemnly, his eyes staring at the street lamps filing off into the distance. "Her name is Janet Tennerman."

"Yeah, that's it. Every boy in my class had a big crush on that lady." Clay stared across at Gifford. "She sure was crazy about you. At least that's what everybody thought."

"The cripple and the PE teacher," Gifford muttered almost bitterly. "Sounds like something Edgar Allen Poe would write if he were alive today."

"I didn't mean to bring up any bad memories for you, Mr. Gifford."

Gifford went on as though he hadn't heard Clay. "We live with the choices we make, Clay. Robert Frost wrote a poem about it, "The Road Not Taken.""

"You read it to us."

"And it does no good to blame our failures on," Gifford grabbed a handful of trousers, lifted his bad leg, and let it drop loosely to the concrete, "the bad breaks we get in this life."

Clay unconsciously rubbed his right elbow, feeling the tenderness where the bones were still mending.

"I have my work of course—and my books," Gifford continued, "and my one great success."

"What's that?"

"You mean *who* don't you?"

Clay rubbed his chin with his left forefinger. "Oh yeah! Leah Daniel."

Gifford smiled, a melancholy pleasure in his eyes. "Yes—Leah. The one big success in all my years of teaching. Scribner's shining new literary star."

"I read her first book. Short stories all about Liberty," Clay added. "I recognized a lot of the people, even if she did give them different names."

"Her second novel's going to be released in the fall." Gifford glanced over at Clay, the hint of a smile on his face. "Did I tell you she dedicated it to me?"

"That's great," Clay responded, seeing how proud Gifford felt that he had had a part in Leah's success. "You sure spent a lot of time with her."

"I gave her the basics, that's all," Gifford admitted. "Dave Stone deserves credit for getting her published."

As though someone had whispered in his ear, Clay felt the evening dwindling down to a kind of sadness. He dreaded the thought of going home and facing his father. "Well, I think I'll go find something to get into. Daddy's gonna chew me out anyway. Might as well make it worthwhile."

"What did you do?"

"Left my welcome-home party that Diane and her mother planned for me." Clay gave Gifford a sheepish grin. "I know Diane's called my house by now."

Gifford felt a twinge of pleasure that someone would snub Dobe Jackson's hospitality. "Why'd you leave?"

Clay remembered listening disinterestedly to the talk of stocks and bonds and annuities as he stood drinking with a small group of men who had satisfied their patriotic fervor by congratulating each other on the sacrifices they were all making for the war effort. "I don't know."

"Well, if you don't want to go home, you can sleep in my living room. I'll throw a quilt and pillow on the couch for you," Gifford offered, putting himself in Clay's position. "Call home first so your mother won't worry herself sick about you. Tell them you're staying over with a friend."

"You sure I wouldn't be putting you out?" Clay brightened at the prospect of a night without a detailed description of how he was ruining his future.

"Not at all." Gifford yawned and glanced at his watch. "I'm sure the night is just beginning for a young man like you, but it's past my bedtime."

"I wouldn't want to disturb you if I get in kinda late," Clay ventured. "I might walk around for a while. I've been kind of— restless lately."

"You won't bother me a bit. Of course neither would a strafing attack by the Japanese once I get to sleep." Gifford pushed off the banister with his good arm. "You'll find a quilt and pillow waiting for you on the living room couch."

"See you in the morning then."

Gifford massaged his bad leg briefly, then walked away, his right foot softly slapping against the concrete. "I'll leave the front door open," he called back over his shoulder.

Clay watched him go, a tragic figure shambling off down the sidewalk. He moved in and out of the amber pools of light from the streetlamps like an actor making his exit at the end of the final act of a play.

Clay knew, however, that Gifford never acted any part, never played to the sympathy of his audience. Just before he turned the corner and disappeared behind a well-trimmed hedge, Clay sensed a nobility about him that he had never seen in any other man.

11

SHORTY'S

Clay left the sidewalks of Liberty behind and strolled along the shoulder of a road that led to the highway, listening to the thick gravel crunch beneath the soles of his shoes. The soft spring air touched his face like a woman's fingertips. A sharp scent of pine filled his nostrils as he gazed upward at the pale moon, gliding through a star-crowded sky. As round and bright as a silver dollar, it bathed the world in a gossamer light.

Reaching the end of the gravel road, Clay turned right and saw Shorty's saloon across the highway from him. Set hard against a kudzu-covered bluff, it had once been a storage shed for hay. Two rough benches sat on either side of the front door along with a Pabst Blue Ribbon sign on the left and a green metal Lucky Strike circle with white lettering on the right.

Crossing the highway, Clay saw a battered and rusty Model T pickup back through a water-filled pothole in the parking lot. Straightening out with a grinding of gears, it clattered off into the night.

As he was about to enter the building, he noticed something glinting in the pale light. Leaning closer, he saw that a knife blade had been driven directly through the center of the Pabst Blue Ribbon sign and broken off. As though it were the natural thing to do, he grasped it with both hands, pulling with all his might. The blade didn't budge. He tried once more, shrugged, and stepped through the door.

"Hey there, Clay. Always glad to have our boys in uniform drop by for a visit." Shorty, who stood over six feet tall, wore his usual overalls and T-shirt. He had the large pale eyes of a fish who spent its life in an underground lake. The anemic light of the barroom gave the place the appearance that it had been submerged in murky water.

Clay walked across the sawdust-covered dirt floor to the bar as Jimmie Rogers wailed "My Carolina Sunshine Girl" from the jukebox. "Good to see you, Shorty. I see you had an interior decorator come in since I was here last."

Always a little slow on the uptake, Shorty protested, "Didn't do no such thing. It's looks too good *already* for the bunch that comes in here."

"You may be right at that."

Lifting a water-beaded bottle of Pabst from a galvanized tub, Shorty popped the cap off in an opener mounted on the side of the bar. "Here you go," he said, handing the bottle to Clay. "Have one on the house."

"Thanks." Clay took the bottle, sitting down on one of the wooden stools. "You about to close up?"

"I was, but take your time. I got nothing waitin' at home but dust and a sink full of dirty dishes."

"Sounds like Edna left you again."

"Yep," Shorty nodded. "That woman don't know how good she's got it."

Clay drank a swallow from the wet bottle rather than responding to Shorty's remark, thinking of the times he had seen Edna downtown with bruises or black eyes. He stared at the jukebox glowing in the dusky room on its platform of scrap lumber. Another Jimmie Rogers record began to play.

"How come you ain't at that homecoming party?" Shorty asked, filling the tub with bottles from a case on the shelf behind him. "Can't be over this early."

"How'd you know about that?"

"Society page," Shorty grinned. "You don't think ol' Dobe would let his precious little daughter as much as sneeze without puttin' it in that newspaper of his, do you?"

"Shorty—you read the society page?"

"Naw—I jest—"

"Yes you do too," Clay interrupted. "It's all over your face. I bet you know all the best gossip from the afternoon teas and bridge parties, too."

Shorty opened his mouth to respond. It stayed open, but no sound came out as he stared at something near the door directly behind Clay.

Turning casually around on his stool, Clay saw two men standing close together just inside the door. The one holding the long-barreled revolver was tall and angular and wore greasy khakis and a striped cap with a short bill. His nervous partner, dressed in a tattered black raincoat and brown fedora, had the shoulders of a lumberjack and the legs of a jockey. Both wore red bandanas tied across their faces in the manner of all good outlaws in the Hoppy and Roy and Gene westerns.

A big smile spread across Clay's face. He immediately thought of the man holding the gun as Roy and his partner as Hoppy. He couldn't have been happier if the two men had been dispatched to deliver him a chest of pirate's gold.

"Wha-whadda you want?" Shorty stood poised with a bottle of beer halfway to the tub.

"We from the First National Bank," the tall man cackled. "We gon' let you make a night deposit. Now ain't that the best service you ever had?"

Shorty, his mouth still open, remained motionless and silent behind the bar.

Hoppy walked around behind the bar. "You deef? Where's the cashbox?"

Before Shorty could answer, Roy screamed at Clay, "Whut you grinning at, soldier boy?"

"Marine." Clay grinned wider. He had wanted to vent the rage building in him since he had returned home, and now the two thieves were like manna from heaven. A thought brushed through the back of his mind that he could get killed, but it seemed trivial in the rush of adrenaline he felt.

"Whut?"

"I'm a Marine, not a soldier," Clay explained calmly. "A man in the *Army* is called a soldier."

Edging around to the end of the bar, Roy squinted his eyes as he tried to figure out why the tall Marine didn't seem at all frightened. He had never seen anyone react this way in any of his other armed robberies and felt that something had gone terribly wrong. "Shut up!"

"Anything you say," Clay replied even more calmly, his smile almost a laugh now.

"Quit *yakking* with that Jarhead and keep that *gun* on him!"

Hoppy growled from behind the bar. "You think this is some kind of *social* hour?"

Shorty had squatted down and taken the cigar box he kept the day's take in from under the bar behind the beer tub. "Here. It's all I got."

Hoppy snatched the box out of Shorty's hand and began rifling through it as though the whole thing were too heavy for him to carry along with him.

Clay yawned and made a stretching motion with both arms, extending the right one holding the beer bottle by its neck as far around as he could reach to give him maximum leverage. His left foot rested solidly on the dirt floor, and his left hand gripped the edge of the bar. He had decided that with his bad elbow, he could get more power with a sidearm throw, whipping his wrist through at the last moment.

Roy glanced at his partner, stuffing dollar bills from the cashbox into his coat pocket. He never saw Clay's arm whip around, sending the beer bottle hurtling through the air toward a spot three inches above the scab on the bridge of his nose.

The heavy bottle thudded with a sickening sound against Roy's forehead. He dropped to the dirt floor like a sack of feed, his revolver landing a foot from his outstretched hand.

Clay turned calmly around on his stool, gazing directly into Hoppy's eyes. "Looks like your friend's sleeping on the job. Reckon the bank'll dock his pay?"

Hoppy glanced at the front door, his eyes wide in disbelief at this sudden turn of events. He thought of the pistol, laying somewhere on the other side of the bar out of sight. Then he glanced back at Clay and put all thoughts of getting to the pistol out of his mind.

Shorty stood up and snatched the box away. "Give me back my money!"

"Why don't you empty your coat pockets, too?" Clay added in a level voice. "And take that silly handkerchief off your face."

The little man reached slowly behind his head to undo his mask, then suddenly bolted toward the end of the bar, making a break for the front door. As he rounded the corner, he stepped quickly over his fallen accomplice and sighted in on the open door to freedom.

As soon as the man broke for the door, Clay slipped off his stool and picked it up in both hands like a baseball bat. Waiting for just the right moment, he hurled it across the room. It caught the little man just above his ankles. Screaming in pain, he tumbled across the dirt floor. He came to rest doubled up, holding onto his damaged legs.

Clay was already standing above him when he scrambled up. He swung a roundhouse right at Clay's head, but missed. As his momentum carried him around, Clay clipped him on the chin with an uppercut.

Standing over the little man's crumpled form, Clay grinned broadly as he turned and glanced over his shoulder at the gunman lying at the end of the bar.

Shorty still clutched his cashbox. "I bet that's the last time them birds mess with us boys from Liberty."

"*Hot dog*, that was fun!" Clay walked over and picked up the heavy revolver from the floor. "Best time I've had since I got back from the Marines."

"You call a holdup fun?"

"It was for *me*," he shrugged, then glanced at the two men on the floor. "They probably wouldn't think so."

"I think they musta put something strange in your head in that Marine Corps, Clay."

Clay laid the pistol on the bar. The rust-pocked blue steel barrel glinted in the dim light. "Nah. They just polished up what I already had."

Shorty walked around the bar, stepped gingerly over the tall man, and squatted down next to the short one. As he retrieved his money from the man's pockets, he glanced over at Clay. "Ain't we gonna get the town marshall out here?"

Clay had a dazed look on his face. "Huh? Oh, yeah—sure. Gimme your truck keys. I'll go down to the jail and fetch him back here."

"What about them?" Shorty asked, glancing at the two unconscious men.

"Let 'em nap."

"They might wake up."

"You got any rope?"

Shorty, having fished all his money from the black raincoat, stood up and walked back behind the bar. Bending down, he fumbled behind some cartons and came up with two lengths of plowline. "That's all I got."

"It'll do."

Clay held out his hand for the keys. Shorty dug deep into his front overalls pocket and handed them to Clay who headed for the front door, tossing the keys into the air and whistling the Marine Corps hymn.

"You really gonna leave me with these two?" Shorty nodded toward the men again.

"Tie 'em up."

"You don't let your shirttail touch you till you get back—you hear?" Shorty hurried over to the tall man, rolled him over on his stomach, and began tying his hands behind his back.

* * *

"Yes, ma'am, I think they fit just fine." Sitting on the low stool next to Ora Peabody, Clay leaned back slightly and admired the chestnut-colored high heels he had just helped her stuff her pudgy feet into.

"Are you *sure* they're not too big?" Ora squinted down at her feet. She resembled Santa Claus's wife from the Coca Cola advertisements, but her husband, bitter from a logging accident that left him crippled, had none of Santa's disposition.

"Oh, no ma'am!" Clay responded quickly, fearing that he would have to prune her toes to get her feet into anything smaller. "They're just right."

"Maybe a seven-and-a-half?"

"They're perfect," Clay shrugged.

"Well—if you say so."

Clay tugged the shoes off and placed them back into the box. "You can pay at the register up front."

Ora pointed to the cash register positioned at the entrance to the shoe department. "What's wrong with that one?"

Clay stared across the bustling aisles of Hightower's Department Store, watching Diane enter through the revolving glass doors.

"Did you hear me, Clayton?"

"Oh, yes, ma'am." Clay handed her the black-and-white box. "I don't know how to work the register."

Ora gave him a puzzled expression.

"I just started this morning." Clay shrugged.

Ora placed the box on her ample lap. "Clayton, you were always a good student. Maybe it's none of my business, but . . ."

Here it comes. The first one.

"Don't you think you should consider your future more?" Ora continued. "Surely you can get into college or a least get a better job until you do."

"Well, this is just temporary, Mrs. Peabody. I'll probably enroll in the fall."

"Good. I'd hate to see you waste your talent, especially since . . ." she glanced at the right arm that hung down the side of his body at a slightly different angle from the left one. "Well, don't let it get you down, Clayton."

"No, ma'am." *You're such a joy to be around. No wonder Euliss always looks like he just swallowed a mouthful of spiders.* "Thanks, and you come back."

Ora tucked the box under her arm and waddled toward the front of the store.

Clay began to clear away the mess in front of Ora's chair where she had tried on sixteen pairs of shoes. As he carried the last boxes back toward the stockroom, he caught Diane's eye. Browsing through a rack of dresses across the wide main aisle from the shoe department, she stared in surprise at Clay.

Disappearing behind the curtains that covered the stockroom door, Clay began reshelving the boxes of shoes. *Maybe she'll go away. . . . No, not Diane.*

Thirty seconds later, Diane's face appeared between the curtains. "Clay, I *thought* that was you back here. What in the world are you doing?"

"Research."

Diane stepped into the long, narrow room. Her black-and-white-checked cotton dress was tailored perfectly for her trim figure, and her blond hair flowed as smoothly as water down to her shoulders. "What?"

"Research," Clay repeated, shoving the boxes back into their slots. "I'm writing a mystery novel about a shoe salesman. It's a murder mystery."

"Since when did you have any interest in books—especially writing them?"

"You know I used to always talk about Leah Daniel and how I'd like to get something published."

"Always? Maybe twice."

"More than that."

Diane put her hands on her hips, tilting her head sideways. "You're not making any sense at all."

"Sure I am," Clay insisted, shoving the last box home. "This is the perfect job for a great plot."

Diane held her position, giving him a skeptical look. "This better be good."

"You see this shoe salesman is really insane." Pulling up a rolling ladder, Clay sat on the third rung. "He hates women because his mama always wanted a little girl and made him wear dresses till he was thirty-four."

"What?"

"Well, maybe twenty-seven or -eight would be better," Clay admitted. "Anyhow—"

"Clay," Diane interrupted. "I've had just about enough of your nonsense!"

"Hold on—it gets better," Clay insisted. "Where was I? Oh yeah, this guy gets it in his head to bump somebody off—so what does he do?"

"I'm leaving right now if you don't stop!"

Clay felt he had to continue his story no matter what happened, knowing that this in itself was as insane as the tale he found himself spinning.

"Clayton? Are you back there?"

Hearing the sound of Ora Peabody's voice, Clay sighed deeply. "Be with you in a minute, Mrs. Peabody."

Diane's eyes glistened with tears. She quickly wiped them away. "Clay—stop this!"

"I'm almost finished," he insisted. "So—our man, having decided on his victim, sells her a pair of shoes—several pairs would be better—that are too tight for her. Like a lot of women, she would never admit they're too small, so she walks around with this excruciating pain until—"

"Stop!" Diane screamed.

"What? You don't like the idea?"

Ora Peabody's plump face appeared between the curtains. "Clayton will you please get out here? I need a smaller size in these shoes you just sold me."

"See what I mean?" Clay whispered to Diane as he stood up. His eyes had taken on a conspiratorial, almost paranoid gleam. "One second, Mrs. Peabody."

"Don't take all day now." Ora's face disappeared.

Clay took a box from the shelf. "The woman with the tight shoes complains so much that it drives her husband nuts, and he murders her."

Diane plopped down on a stepladder, leaning over with her face in her hands.

Clay left through the curtains and returned in five minutes with the same pair of shoes. "You all right, sweetheart?"

Diane looked up, her eyes red and swollen. "Clay, what's wrong with you?"

Slamming the box against the wall, Clay responded, "I don't know."

"Why did you leave your job at the lumberyard?"

"Hartley fired me."

Diane stood up and walked over to him. "You've just got to go to work at Daddy's newspaper. I can't understand why you're so set against it."

Clay stared down at the linoleum floor.

"You worked there in high school."

"I didn't have any choice then." He glanced up at her. "Your daddy despises me, Diane. The only reason he tolerates me at all is because of you."

"Don't be silly. Daddy's gruff with everybody—just about." Feeling the hollowness of her words, Diane tried to smile as though that would give them credibility. "If you'd just show him a little respect, I'm sure things would work out between the two of you. Won't you at least try?"

Clay shrugged and continued to stare at the floor, rubbing the top of his right hand with his left palm.

Diane glanced about the cluttered stockroom. "Clay, you've got to get out of here."

Looking up at her with a puzzled frown he asked, "What do you mean—quit my job?"

"Exactly."

"It's honest work."

Diane stood up, giving Clay's workplace another disdainful look as she walked toward the curtained doorframe.

"Well—what's wrong with selling shoes?"

"It *is* honest work," Diane agreed, "but it's *not* what I want for my husband."

"It's not exactly *my* dream job either, Diane." Clay clasped his right elbow with his left hand. "But people don't always get what they want in this life."

"Some don't. But then again some do." Diane leaned against the wall next to the door, giving Clay a coy smile.

"What's that supposed to mean?"

"You *do* want to marry me—don't you?"

Clay felt himself being lured into something that would change his life completely, like an animal toward the trapper's springed steel.

"Don't you?"

"Sure."

"Well then, you'll just have to leave all this," Diane flicked her hand at the room, "and go to work for Daddy."

Clay gazed stonily at her. "You think blackmail is a sound foundation for a marriage?"

"Oh, hush! That's a *dreadful* thing to say," Diane shot back huffily.

"What is it then?"

Diane stood up straight, her arms folded across her breast. "It's a wife wanting her husband to have a respectable job."

"Work for your father, huh?"

"You make it sound like I'm asking you to go to work picking cotton."

Clay felt he would be much happier dragging a cotton sack behind him in the broiling sun than being under Dobe Jackson's thumb all day.

"Well, what's your answer?" Diane had balled her hands into fists, placing them on her hips.

"Sydney or the Bush, huh?"

"What are you babbling about now?" Diane asked, irritation at the forefront of her voice. "I declare, sometimes I think you lost your brain somewhere out in that Pacific Ocean."

"Just an expression I picked up down in Australia," Clay explained, thinking that perhaps Diane wasn't far wrong about his mental state.

Diane continued to stare at him, her face becoming slowly flushed with anger.

"Absolutely, my precious." Clay felt he was betraying some long-forgotten ideal with his words. "Maybe ol' Dobe and me will be best buddies before it's all over."

"Oh, Clay, that's wonderful!" Diane rushed into his arms, kissing him on both cheeks and the mouth.

12

A CHEAP PIECE OF JUNK

"Do you think it's going all right so far?" Diane sat on the satin coverlet of her antique four-poster among a dozen or so stuffed animals.

Her older sister Peggy sat next to her, brushing her shiny red hair. "Good as any other engagement party I've ever been to. They all simply bore me to death."

"Oh, you think you're so sophisticated now that you've worked up in Washington for a year," Diane pouted. "It's just *got* to turn out OK after what happened at his homecoming party. I'll just *die* if he messes up this time."

Peggy lay the brush down and straightened the straps of her jade green dress. "I'll say one thing for Clay, he always was a handsome devil: tall as a silo and those shoulders are simply dreamy."

"I asked you about the *party*, Peggy!" Diane snapped. "I already know what Clay *looks* like!"

Peggy dismissed her sister's complaint. "Oh, don't be so jealous! He's *much* too young for me."

"It looks like almost everybody I invited showed up," Diane offered.

"And some that you *didn't* invite."

"Like who?"

"Like Angela Spain for one."

"I could just shoot Daddy for that!" Diane slapped the bedspread with the flat of her hand.

"*He* invited her?"

"No, but . . ."

"I didn't think Mama would let him get away with that," Peggy interrupted.

"As I was saying, he invited Lila Kronen as a gesture of

149

friendship to his opposition and told her she could bring a friend. So who does she bring?"

"None other than the infamous Angela Spain."

"Right."

"I don't think she's any worse than some others in this town who shall remain nameless."

"You're probably right." Diane grinned mischievously. "But she was always so—indiscreet. Everybody and his brother knew she was running around on poor ol' Morton."

"That's certainly true. I suppose guile is something that takes a lot of practice to really get right." Peggy stared thoughtfully at a huge white Teddy bear propped against the headboard. "Angela never was much good at it, was she?"

"Maybe she just didn't care." Diane slipped off the bed and straightened her skirt. "Anyway, I hear she's got religion now. Isn't that the cat's meow?"

"Angela got religion? *That'll* be the day." Peggy stood up and gave herself a final once-over in the dresser mirror. "We better be getting back. You don't want to leave Clay alone too long in the same house with Angela Spain."

"Oh, you!" Diane picked the brush up from the bed and tossed it at her sister.

* * *

"You better take it easy on that stuff, Mr. Clay." Cletus reluctantly poured another double shot of bourbon into Clay's heavy glass.

"I'm sober as a judge, Cletus," Clay replied, leaning both elbows on the bar as he surveyed the same crowd that attended his homecoming party milling about wearing silks and satins and summer tuxedos. At Diane's insistence, he had worn his Marine dress uniform again. "Judge Roy Bean that is."

"You 'member what happened last time," Cletus reminded him, shoving the glass across the bar. "Mr. Dobe won't stand for nothin' like that agin."

Clay downed the whiskey in one gulp. Letting his breath out with a hissing sound, he felt the liquid burn all the way down to his stomach. But he thought there wasn't enough liquor in the whole town to rid him of an image from the past month that kept playing over and over in his mind like a record stuck in the same spot.

Clay had given in to Diane's badgering and gone to her father's office at the *Liberty Herald* to ask for a job. After a two-hour wait, he had been ushered into the plush office where Jackson made him wait another ten minutes while he handled a phone call and sorted through some paperwork.

Gazing at Clay with a smug and condescending smile on his face, Jackson had spoken in his best "paternal benevolence" voice. "It's about time you came to your senses, Clayton. Now that baseball's no longer an option, you have to get on with your life."

"Yes, sir."

"I'm not cutting you any slack just because my daughter's infatuated with you."

Our engagement party's coming up, Clay thought. *You call that infatuation?* "I don't expect any."

"Good, we understand each other then."

Clay had nodded.

"Be at the loading ramp at three o'clock Monday morning," Jackson had said in a voice fraught with sarcasm. "You'll drive the delivery truck for the commercial accounts. The first time you're late will be your last."

Clay knew that the job he had been given was usually filled by men with limited abilities and was known to be a dead-end street as far as advancement with the newspaper went. "I'll be there."

Jackson had returned to his paperwork without a word as though Clay no longer existed.

Along with the whiskey, Clay felt the anger burning with a hotter flame in the pit of his stomach. The past weeks had been torture for him with Jackson or one of his toadies constantly badgering him on the job. He finished his drink and turned toward Cletus for another.

"Hello, Clay. Lovely party." Angela Spain, wearing a lavender blouse with a lace collar and a long white skirt, walked over next to him.

Clay glanced at her. "Yeah."

"You don't seem particularly pleased for someone who's getting engaged to such a lovely girl."

Scowling at her now, Clay inexplicably felt the anger rising again in his chest. It seemed to glow inside his brain, causing thoughts that he couldn't seem to shackle. "What do you know about how I feel? You don't know anything about me."

Puzzled and a little hurt at Clay's reaction, Angela turned away. "May I have a Coke please?"

"Yes ma'am," Cletus grinned, his teeth dazzling against his dark skin. "You look nice, Miss Angela."

"Thank you." Angela took a swallow of her Coke and turned to leave.

"It's her job to look nice—isn't it, Angela?" Clay sneered down at her.

"I'm afraid I don't understand."

"Oh, she understands all right," Clay grinned maliciously toward Cletus.

"You've had too much to drink, Clay," Angela offered in a soft voice. "Maybe you should lie down for a while."

"Now that's something you know all about, isn't it, *Mrs. Spain*?" Angela had never offended Clay in any way, but he couldn't seem to control the rage that had begun to spill out of him. "Lying down, that is—even if it's only for one-hour intervals."

Angela knew that people had talked about her behind her back for years, but no one had ever confronted her with her transgressions face to face. Even though it hurt terribly, somehow this was better. To her surprise, she felt no desire to strike back at her accuser.

Clay expected something other than this calm exterior presented to him by Angela. Directionless, his rage seemed to intensify as it sought a target.

Angela turned to leave the bar, but was stopped by Clay's next volley.

"Ol' Morton didn't know what he was gettin' himself into when he married this one," Clay glanced over at Cletus, then leered at Angela. "Did he now?"

"No," she replied quietly, "he didn't."

Clay had lost control now, his thoughts following no course of logic whatsoever. "I'll bet that little sailor boy wished he had never left El Paso."

Angela's eyes grew suddenly glassy with tears. "Excuse me,

please." She hurried off across the terrace toward the bright squares of the French doors.

"That was awful ugly, Mr. Clay."

Clay watched Angela enter into the brightly lit drawing room. "Some people just got no sense of humor, Cletus."

"Nothin' funny a'tall in what you said."

"Oh, come on, Cletus. Take it easy." Clay shoved his glass across the bar. "Hit me again."

"You wouldn't like what I'd hit you with." Cletus turned and walked to the other end of the bar.

*   *   *

"And don't you ever set foot in this house again, you ungrateful low-life drunk!" Dobe Jackson stood at his front door, rubbing his bruised jaw as he watched Keith Demerie, Taylor Spain and Hartley Lambert drag Clay down the circular driveway and across the freshly clipped lawn.

The three men heaved Clay down the steep slope. He tumbled sideways until he hit the street gutter at the bottom, groaned, and lay still.

"That'll teach you to talk to decent people that way," Hartley Lambert called out. "You oughta take some lessons from your daddy. At least he knows his place in this town."

Clay watched the three men turn and walk out of sight beyond the edge of the slope. With some effort, he managed to sit up, turn around, and lean back on the damp grass with one elbow. Taking his handkerchief from his back pocket, he gingerly wiped the blood away from the cut above his left eyebrow and his battered lips. One tooth felt loose when he touched it.

His head fuzzy with drink as well as the beating he had taken at the hands of the four men, Clay found that he was unable to reconstruct the events of the night. He vaguely remembered talking with Angela Spain and that he had hurt her feelings. After that— only a blur of motion, the sounds of men shouting at him, and the pain of fists pounding his face and hard shoes slamming into his ribs after he was down.

Clay lay back on the slope of the lawn, closing his eyes to fight off the nausea that was beginning to sweep over him. He felt revulsion at himself for what he had said to Angela and for the way he had behaved toward the others even though he could remember most of it only in bits and pieces.

"Clay . . ."

Pushing himself upright, Clay opened his eyes and glanced around.

"Over here."

Clay rubbed is eyes with both hands. As his vision cleared, he saw Diane standing only a few feet away next to a huge pine, almost lost in its deep shadow. Putting his hands at his sides, he leaned forward to get up.

"No—stay where you are!"

"I can barely see you," Clay muttered painfully through his swollen lips.

"Doesn't matter," Diane replied coldly. "This will only take a moment."

Clay ran his hands through his hair, pushing it back out of his eyes. "I really messed up good this time, didn't I? Well, I learned my lesson for sure and—"

"No!" Diane cut him off sharply. "I don't care if you learned anything or not."

"What are you talking about?"

"It's over."

"Oh, come on now, baby," Clay tried to sound as though he had merely used the wrong fork at dinner. "Don't make such a big deal out of this."

"I'm not making a big deal out of anything. You've done it all yourself."

With his head still spinning slowly and his vision blurry, Clay felt as though he were talking with a disembodied voice from the shadows. "Will you please come on over here so we can talk, Diane? This is stupid."

"I agree—and you've brought it all on yourself."

Clay's voice had a raspy sound from the harsh whiskey. The blood on his lips was becoming crusty, making it hard for him to form the words. "Diane, I'm sorry for whatever it was I did. I just don't remember much."

"You called my father a pompous . . . I can't even repeat what you called him. And you insulted Keith Demerie because he didn't go in the service."

Sounds like I was just telling the truth. "Well, whatever I did, I apologize."

"It's much too late for that. My family and I have run out of patience with you."

"But—what about our engagement—all the plans we made?" Clay pleaded, feeling that he was losing his last hope for straightening out his life.

"Here's what I think of our engagement!"

Clay saw a quick brightness as the ring arced through the air and hit him in the chest.

"I never should have accepted such a cheap piece of junk anyway!" Diane whirled around, her dress a brief flash against the shadows, and disappeared.

Lying back against the cool grass, Clay felt his head gradually beginning to clear, but as he returned to full consciousness the pain intensified. *Serves me right. I should have been blown to bits on Tarawa. So many good men were lost—men that had wives and children and jobs, good reasons to go on living.*

Clay listened to the sounds of music and laughter drifting out from the party behind him. From beyond the house, the band began to play "I'll Never Smile Again"; the sentimental melody sounded like the dream of a song in the distance.

The song took Clay back to the day he had left for the Marine Corps. Waving at him from the station platform, Diane had just disappeared from sight as he continued to gaze out the window at the last fleeting sights of Liberty. Four soldiers on their way to a replacement depot on the East Coast had formed an impromptu quartet in his car and had sung the Sinatra hit. The whole car had applauded at the end, making one request after the other until the men finally had to beg off with hoarse voices.

As Clay listened to the song, immersed in the tormenting memories, he could see nothing left that was worth living for. He struggled painfully to his knees, then stood up and waited until his head cleared. Brushing himself off, he straightened his tie, and walked off toward town, following his shadow from one streetlight to another.

* * *

"You shore saved *my* hide, boy!" Shorty opened a wet bottle of Pabst, and set it on the bar in front of Clay. "I heard them same two boys killed a feller at a service station in the next county the same night they come in here. If it wasn't for you, I'd be pushing up daisies out there in the boneyard."

"Yeah. I heard the same thing," Clay muttered through his blood-crusted lips. "If I'd known they really meant business, I might have made another door in your back wall getting out of here instead of acting like a fool."

Shorty squinted up at Clay as he washed glasses in a dishpan below the bar. "You ain't fooling me none, Clay McCain. I seen the kind of men who run from a fight, which is most of 'em, and you just ain't got it in you. You enjoyed every minute of looking down that gun barrel."

Clay knew what Shorty said was true. He also knew that it had nothing to do with courage. The feeling that had possessed him that night was one of simply not caring what happened to him. And then there was that feeling like no other when he released the rage burning inside of him, as though someone had turned a pressure valve just before the critical point was reached.

Shorty spoke into his dishpan. "You a sorry sight now if I ever seen one though."

Clay touched his left eye, almost swollen shut. Shorty had cleaned the blood off him and pulled the cut above the eye closed as best he could with adhesive tape. His lips had begun to bleed again as soon as they were cleaned. "I reckon I deserved everything they did to me."

"What did you do—if I'm not meddlin' too much?" Shorty asked hesitantly.

"That's the real pitiful part of this whole mess," Clay laughed bitterly. "I don't even remember."

"Nothing?"

"I said some nasty things to a few people," Clay admitted. "But then I've done that on a pretty regular basis ever since I got back home."

"Maybe you oughta just stay plumb away from parties. I think you're allergic to 'em."

Clay laughed, then stopped abruptly as his lips burned with pain. "I guess you're right."

"Your folks know where you are?" Shorty glanced at the pale amber glow of the Camel Cigarettes clock above the jukebox. "It's past midnight. You better get on home."

"Already been there."

Shorty stepped into the tiny storage room behind the bar, coming directly out with a case of beer.

"Dad kicked me out," Clay continued. "Said he'd had enough of my foolishness."

Shorty began filling the tub with beer.

"I think he's afraid that ol' Hartley's gonna fire him if he sides with me."

"Yeah," Shorty mumbled into his tub, "him and Dobe's big buddies."

Clay stared thoughtfully at the jukebox. "Guess I've got something in common with Ben Logan."

"You mean besides being a war hero?"

"War hero—me?" Clay muttered. "I ain't fit to stand in Ben Logan's shadow."

"They don't give Silver Stars away for door prizes," Shorty objected. "Not in the *Marines* they don't."

Clay shook his head slowly. "Doesn't matter anyway—none of it. What I'm talking about is Ben and I both got dumped by the daughters of the two richest men in town."

Shorty leaned on the bar with both of his milky-colored forearms. "That's the gospel truth," he agreed. "But look how Ben come out of it."

"You mean Rachel?"

"Yep. If he'd hooked up with Debbie Lambert—I wouldn't give you two cents for that marriage. But a man couldn't ask for a better wife than Rachel."

Clay continued to stare at the jukebox.

"Same thing could happen to you."

"I wouldn't count on that." Clay ran his hands though his hair and leaned his elbows on the bar.

"Where you stayin' tonight?"

"Beats me."

"I'd ask you over to the house," Shorty hesitated, staring

down at the duckboards resting on the dirt floor. "Well, Edna come back, and it's kinda touch-and-go at the house right now. You know how women are."

"No, I don't think I know much about women at all," Clay mumbled.

"Tell you what." Shorty stepped back and frowned into his storage room. "Nah."

"Nah? What do mean, *Nah?*" Clay leaned over the bar, trying to see what Shorty was looking at.

Shaking his head, Shorty stepped back to the bar. "Want another whiskey?"

"Not now. What were you talking about?"

"I was gonna say you could stay here in the storage room until you found something, but—"

"But nothing, I'll take it," Clay insisted. "It's either that or a bed of pine straw under a tree somewhere."

"It ain't much."

"Good, it'll be perfect for me then," Clay declared bluntly, "'cause I ain't much either."

"You better come around here and take a look before you make your mind up so quick."

Clay walked painfully around behind the bar, stepping to the door of the storage room. Glancing inside he saw cases of beer and whiskey stacked almost to the ceiling in most of the cramped space of the room. Dirt and grime seemed to have taken the place of paint on the parts of the walls that were visible. The low ceiling was rapidly rusting tin that had begun flaking onto the dirt floor and the bare striped ticking of a mattress and pillow.

As he stepped into the cramped confines of the room, Clay heard a rough scratching along the far wall and something heavy banging against the tin roof. Squinting in the dim light, he saw a wood rat that looked as big as a good-sized cat scurry through the opening between the tin and the ceiling joist.

"Maybe sleeping underneath a pine tree won't be all *that* bad," Clay muttered, stepping back out of the tiny room.

"Well, it ain't nothing fancy, but it'll keep you dry if it rains," Shorty offered, touting the room's best feature. "There's a blanket under here somewhere."

While Shorty rummaged around behind some boxes beneath

the bar, Clay glanced back inside the storage room, wondering how his life had come to such a sad state in a little more than two years.

Shorty finished his nightly chores, tucked his cashbox under his arm, and headed for the door. "I won't be here until ten in the morning so don't worry about getting up. I fixed the jukebox so you can play all the songs you want for free."

"Thanks."

"Help yourself to anything you want to drink. I'll bring you some biscuits or something in the morning." With a nod of his head, Shorty walked out into the parking lot.

Clay heard Shorty's pickup grind slowly at first, then faster. Finally the engine sputtered to life. With a creaking of springs and the clanging of scrap metal in the bed, it jounced through the parking lot and onto the highway.

Well, it ain't much, but it's home. Clay surveyed the dimly lighted tavern and hefted a full bottle of whiskey from the shelf. Wandering over to the jukebox, he studied the selections a few minutes before he punched in Tommy Dorsey's "Boogie Woogie," Glenn Miller's "In the Mood" and four other instrumentals. *Nothing with words for me. Keeps down the old memory quotient.*

Raking a chair to him with his foot, Clay sat down and leaned back, crossing his legs on top of the table. *Yes, sir, I gotta, 'Keep gloom down to a minimum.'* He sang to the lyrics of a current pop tune into the gloomy loneliness of the room.

Part 4

THE END
OF THE STORM

13

ROCK BOTTOM

Sunlight streamed through the windows, giving the room a pale gold brilliance that hurt Clay's eyes as he struggled up from a nightmarish darkness. He blinked, his eyes watering in the glare, then sat up, trying to rub the cobwebs of sleep from his eyes. After the light, the first thing he noticed was the fresh clean smell and softness of the sheets and the pale yellow pajamas he had on. He knew they had been dried on a clothesline because he could still smell the sun in them.

Sitting up in the bed, he put a pillow behind him, leaning back against the headboard. A pitcher of water and bottles of patent medicine sat on the nightstand. Furnished with a cherrywood dresser, a cedar chest at the foot of the bed, and a Queen Anne chair, the room was comfortable and inviting.

Noticing a door that led to a tiled bath, Clay eased his legs over the edge of the bed. His head swam and he felt sick at his stomach. When he tried to stand, he felt that the arches of his feet would no longer support his weight. Finally standing up, he had to hold on to the bedpost to maintain his balance.

Walking unsteadily to the bathroom, he flicked on the light and stepped in front of the lavatory. The image in the mirror sent a chill through him. At first he thought it was somehow the reflection of someone behind him, but he quickly realized that was impossible.

Clay saw the dark hollow eyes staring out at him from a gaunt, almost emaciated-looking face. A heavy stubble could not hide the yellow pallor of his skin overlaid with several dark crusty scabs and blotchy ridges that looked like mosquito bites. His teeth appeared coated with a green fungus and his hair, although it had been washed, stuck out in all directions.

After washing his face, Clay took a new toothbrush from the medicine cabinet and brushed his teeth. He wet and combed his hair, then rubbed the heavy stubble on his cheeks. He decided he was still too shaky to risk using the safety razor that lay on a glass shelf in the cabinet and walked slowly back to the bed, breathing as though he had run wind sprints.

Still too disoriented and weak to be concerned about where he was, Clay only knew that he somehow felt safe. He had just dozed off when he heard footsteps in the narrow hallway that led to the living area and kitchen. A faint scent of gardenia drifted like a fond memory in the bright air of the room.

Slowly opening his eyes, Clay thought that he was surely lost in a dream. He saw a soft cloud of dark hair and violet eyes that soothed his hurts by their mere presence and a smile that radiated warmth as surely as the sunshine.

"Oh, good, you're awake. I was afraid you were going to sleep twenty years like Rip Van Winkle."

Clay opened his mouth to speak, but only a raspy grunt escaped his dry, scratchy throat.

Angela poured a glass of water from the white ceramic pitcher. "Here, you sound all dried out."

Clay took the glass, turning it up to his mouth and draining it. The water felt like a healing balm as it cooled his throat and stomach. He hadn't realized how very thirsty he was. "Thanks."

Pulling a cushioned chair covered in a striped velvet fabric near the bed, Angela sat down, saying nothing, only gazing at Clay with a pleasant noncommittal expression on her face.

Clay took in her pale green dress made of soft cotton that contoured Angela's body in graceful flowing folds. "How long have I been here?"

"Three days."

"How did I get here?" Clay remembered little since that first night at Shorty's. The days and nights had simply been a blend of morning quiet when he and Shorty had talked, afternoon noise as the tavern grew continually more crowded until closing time, and silent nights, when Clay again found himself alone with only a bottle and a jukebox for company.

His nights on the cot in the storage room had been filled with nightmares and dreams too painful to remember when he had awakened to take several harsh mouthfuls of whiskey and lie down again to stare at rats that were actually in the room with him—and at some that were not.

"Amos found you lying under one of the big pine trees at the back of the property, unconscious." Angela took the glass and poured some more water.

Sipping the water, Clay gazed into Angela's eyes. "I-I can't remember when the party was—the one . . ."

"Ten days ago."

"I have to call home."

"I've already done that," Angela said, her voice hardly above a whisper.

Gradually Clay began to remember the scene at the party with Angela and how badly he had mistreated her. He couldn't hold her eyes as he spoke. "I-I hope you'll forgive me for the way I treated you at the party. It was a terrible thing to do! I don't even know why I acted like that. You've always been nice to me."

Angela smiled, shaking her head slowly. "Don't worry about it. I'm surprised you remember it at all."

"How did I . . ." Clay glanced down at the pajamas.

Angela's quick laugh sounded musical in the stillness of the room. "Amos."

"Who?"

"He's the handyman who's worked here for years. He cleaned you up."

"Where's my uniform?"

"At the cleaners," Angela replied, noticing Clay's modesty. "I'll pick it up later today."

"I guess I'd better get up and get out of here. Don't want to bother you any more."

"I don't think you're strong enough to leave yet." Angela stood up and walked away, stopping at the door. "Just stay in bed. I'll be right back."

"But I can't stay in your house." Clay found himself strangely uneasy in Angela's presence.

"You needn't be concerned about that." Angela laughed again. "This is an apartment above the garage. It's completely separate from the house."

Clay watched Angela disappear down the hall. He felt like a

child again, not only from being so weak, but because he was experiencing the same emotions he had felt as a boy when his mother had
taken care of him after he had disobeyed her and gotten into trouble.

Angela appeared in less than a minute carrying a white wicker
tray. She walked over to the bedside and placed it in front of Clay,
resting the legs on either side of him. "Here you are. Eat as much as
you can."

Clay stared down at a large white bowl of vegetable beef soup
with crackers and a large glass of milk. Taking a spoonful, he tried
it carefully. It tasted rich and nourishing and delicious with just
enough seasoning to bring out the flavor of the fresh vegetables.
"This is great! Better than my mama used to make, and I thought
hers was the best in the world."

"Thank you."

"You made this?"

Angela nodded, never in her wildest dreams believing that she
would get such pleasure from watching a man eat. She could almost taste the pleasure that Clay got from every bite, could almost
feel the nourishing soup mending his injuries and putting strength
back into his malnourished and alcohol-damaged body. "I'm so
glad you like it. I never did much cooking before, but lately it's
something that I've come to enjoy."

"You oughta open a restaurant," Clay mumbled between
mouthfuls. Then, remembering where he was, said apologetically,
"But why would you need to, right?"

When Clay had finished, he breathed a deep sigh. "That was
the best tasting soup I've ever had."

Angela smiled her thanks again.

"I really gotta get out of here now. How can I ever pay you
back for what you've done for me?" Clay set the tray aside and
tried to stand up. But the room swam before his eyes, and he carefully lay back down.

"You stay right where you are." Angela took the tray away,
returning with a bottle of white pills. Shaking one out, she handed
it to Clay along with a glass of water.

"What's this?"

"I don't know. Ollie gave them to me when I told him what
condition you were in. He said you should take one three times a
day and stay in bed for three or four more days."

"I can't stay here."

"You most certainly *can*."

Clay felt his face grow slightly hot. "But what would people say about you?"

"Nothing they haven't already." Angela took the glass and placed it on the nightstand. Pulling the covers around Clay's chest, she said, "You just rest and let me worry about what people will say. I'll have Amos come up later and help you with your bath. What do you want for supper?"

Clay felt too weak to protest anything that Angela said. "Anything—as long as you cook it."

* * *

"You sho' been a big help to me, Mr. Clay." Amos Chaney leaned on his Kaiser blade, his blue shirt and overalls stained darkly with sweat. Then his face clouded over slightly as he asked, "It ain't none of my business, but I seed that big scar on yo' back and them little un's in yo' chest all week now. What done something like that to you?"

With a bitter smile, Clay pointed to the cluster of jagged white scars beneath his right breastbone. "The Japs gave me these little souvenirs."

"Is all them little bullet holes?"

"Something like that. It's called shrapnel. A mortar round exploded right next to me."

"What about yo' back?"

"The Navy doctor did that taking the Jap souvenirs out."

"I ain't never been to no war. Thank the Lawd for dat," Amos mumbled, his head bowed slightly.

Clay sat down on the pine needles and leaned back against the rough bark of the tree. "This is just what I needed, Amos. Sweat out all that poison I've been putting into my body for the last three or four months."

Amos sat down against a tree next to Clay. "We'll have dis place looking like it ought to in no time wid both of us working at it—sho will."

Clay gazed at the briars and weeds that had grown up in the little glade at the back of Angela's property. "How'd it get away from you like this?"

"Took sick in that last little cold snap back at the end of March. Took me three or fo' months to get shed of whatever it was I got. My chest still burns like fire if I get too winded." Amos smiled at the wild growth in the glade. "Don't take long for wild things to take over if you jes' turn 'em loose on their own."

"How long you been working for the Spains?" Working with Amos took Clay back to the times when he had worked with Cletus Felder at the lumbermill. The satisfying feeling he had was the same—that of any man who gives an honest day's work for his pay. He wondered if he could ever feel at ease with men who didn't earn their living by hard labor.

"Little more'n twenty years." Amos took a white handkerchief from his back pocket and wiped his face. The color of coffee and cream, his skin was freckled with brown spots half the size of dimes. "Mr. Morton never paid no mo' attention to me than he did a stray cat. Never treated me bad neither."

"How about Angela?"

"She wudn't no more than a child when she married Mr. Morton. Jest a pretty little girl," Amos grinned. "She sho' turned into a fine lady this last year though. Couldn't ask for a nicer, kinder lady than she is."

Clay picked up a quart bottle of water that sat against the side of the tree. It was filled with ice cubes and beaded with cool drops of condensation. Turning it up, he drank half of it without taking it from his lips. "Ahhh, that's good. Well, I guess we'd better get on back to work."

Amos drank from his own jar. "How long you reckon you'll be helping me out here?"

"Don't know." Clay picked up the long-handled blade and lay into the high, thick stand of weeds. He swung it exactly as he had his bat, swinging for the fence on a high hard one. Working next to Amos gave Clay a sense of belonging although he didn't understand why.

As he worked, Clay kept Angela's image on the front steps of his mind. He could almost smell her fragrance, almost see the graceful sway of her body as she strolled along next to him on their late afternoon walks beneath the purple shadows of the ancient trees.

Angela had begun to be a part of his very being and the

memory of her face would see him through those hours past midnight when he could almost smell the cordite, could almost hear the clattering of heavy machine guns—when the blood of his friends flowed again onto the blackened earth of Tarawa.

* * *

He certainly seems a kind and gentle man—now that he's no longer drinking. I guess losing baseball was about the worst thing that could have happened to him, even though he never mentions it. As soon as he sets a direction for himself in life he'll make some woman a . . . well, that's none of my business. Angela sat at the big wooden desk in the reception area of the *Journal* typing J.T.'s latest column from his scratchy handwriting.

"Angela, could you step in here for a moment?" Lila peeked around the edge of her frosted-glass door.

"Sure thing." Angela typed a final sentence and entered the office.

"Well, you certainly brighten things up around here," Lila smiled, glancing at Angela's summer dress printed with pale blue and green flowers.

Angela smoothed her dress out as she sat down in a leather chair next to Lila's desk. "It's been so awfully hot lately, seems like the bright colors keep my mind off the heat."

"I just want you to know how much I appreciate your helping out around here." Lila stared at the bright window where a warm breeze stirred the diaphanous curtains.

"Oh, you don't have to thank me," Angela said in mild protest. "This has been one of the best things that's happened to me in a long time. I finally feel like I'm doing something worthwhile."

"That's certainly true," Lila replied with conviction. "I get more calls about J.T.'s articles than anything else. And we both know who's writing them."

"Why—J.T. is."

Lila smiled knowingly at Angela. "I've seen those notes of his that you type from. I have to admit that he knows how to collect some colorful information, but making a coherent news article out of them is an entirely different matter."

Angela blushed slightly.

"J.T.'s great verbally," Lila went on, "but he hasn't got the discipline or the inclination to put in the hard work it takes to get something ready for the presses."

"Well, I certainly couldn't do what he does—just go out there cold to homes and businesses and get people to open up their lives," Angela admitted.

"J.T. *is* good at that all right," Lila agreed. "He's certainly got the gift of gab. But even more than that, he genuinely cares about people—and they can tell."

Lila smoothed her hair and fidgeted with the cameo she wore on her linen jacket.

"What's really on your mind, Lila? It must be pretty serious." Angela had noticed how her brow was knitted with concern when she first entered the office.

"The same thing that's been there all along, I suppose." She gazed through the window at two fox squirrels chasing each other in quick spirals around the thick trunk of the oak. "Having to close down the *Journal*."

Angela was surprised by her answer. "I thought you were doing much better!"

"Oh, we are," Lila admitted quickly. "But it's still not enough for the paper to make it on its own. I've been making up for the losses all along, but now my savings are exhausted."

"I've got some money!" Angela said ardently. "I'll be glad to help you out!" Then she leaned back in her chair, speaking more softly. "Morton was more than generous. I could never spend all that he left me."

Lila felt the warm flow of friendship, almost a living thing, from Angela. "That's awfully kind of you, Angela, but this is something that I have to do on my own."

"Aren't you selling enough papers?"

"We are under normal circumstances. But Dobe Jackson's offered my people more money than I could ever pay them—just to put me out of business." Lila shook her head slowly. "Of course when the competition's gone, he'll fire them all because he doesn't really need them in the first place. Right now, though, all they can see is that big paycheck."

"There must be *something* we can do."

"If I had another good man or two who knew something about

the newspaper business—layout, running the press, selling advertisements. Dobe's got them all sewn up though." Lila began to sort through some invoices on her desk. "In a couple of weeks, all that will be left is Henry and me."

"We just *can't* let this happen!" Angela assured Lila, her mouth set in determination. "I don't know how, but we've *got* to keep this paper going."

"I didn't expect you to be this upset about it, Angela," Lila remarked, a perplexed look on her face. "I guess I didn't know how much it meant to you."

Angela stood up and walked to the window where the breeze stirred her soft hair. "We're fighting a war for freedom. How can we just stand by and let a man like Dobe Jackson take over like he *owns* this town? You've got as much right to publish a newspaper as he does."

"Maybe you've forgotten something in your fervor for the *Journal*, Angela."

Angela turned to face Lila, a puzzled expression on her face. "What's that?"

"Dobe's got rights, too, which means he can use any *legal* means to put me out of business."

"But that's not fair."

"Yes it is." Lila smiled at Angela's passion to keep her in business. "This nation's economy is based on free enterprise. And I'd much rather see things the way they are than to have the alternative."

"Alternative?"

"Yes—government subsidies, which means government control of our businesses. That's when we truly lose our freedom. The next step would be some federal bureaucrat telling me what I can and can't print."

"I hadn't look at it that way."

That's exactly what happened under Hitler. People depended on government, in the form of der Führer, to be like a big daddy to them—to take care of all their needs. Well the price you pay for that is total loss of freedom."

Again Angela felt like a student in class rather than just a friend of Lila's.

"No sir," Lila continued passionately, "I'll take an old rascal like Dobe Jackson any day over some petty Washington lackey whose head would probably split wide open if an original thought ever got close to it."

"OK," Angela laughed. "We won't let anybody with a cardboard briefcase in the door."

"Agreed." Lila felt much better about the problems she faced now that she had shared them with Angela.

"But," Angela spoke with renewed determination, "we're going to keep this newspaper in business."

*   *   *

"You've just got to help her out, Clay!" Angela sat with him on the flagstone terrace behind the house. She had returned from the offices of the *Journal* just as the sun had vanished suddenly behind a distant stand of mimosa, leaving the sultry air bathed in a rose-colored glow.

Clay, his hair still wet from his shower, sat across from her drinking a tall glass of lemonade. He wore a clean white T-shirt and faded jeans, his long legs stretched out, bare feet resting on the cool smooth stone. "I don't know, Angela."

"But you already know about the newspaper business, and Dobe Jackson's stolen everybody else away from her." Angela poured herself some lemonade from the heavy glass pitcher she had brought outside.

Clay moved his glass slowly around in front of him, listening to the soft chinking of the ice cubes.

"Well?"

"I wouldn't be any good at it, Angela," Clay protested. "I've messed up at every job I've tried."

Angela stood up, frustrated by Clay's apathetic demeanor. "What are you going to do then? Give up on your whole life at the age of twenty?"

Taking a long swallow of his drink, Clay stared up at a bullbat flitting about erratically in the darkening air. "I just wouldn't want anybody depending on me."

Sitting back down, Angela crossed her legs and folded her arms across her breast. "I, I, I—me, me, me. That pretty well sums up your whole attitude, I guess."

Surprised at Angela's sudden anger, Clay stared at her face, almost lost in shadow. Still, he could see that her eyes held an intense light. "Why are you so mad at me? It's not like I promised to help Lila out of her trouble."

"No . . . you didn't, did you?" Angela stood up again and the last light gleamed in her hair. "I just realized myself why I'm so angry, Clay. Maybe it doesn't even have to do with Lila."

Clay watched Angela's graceful movements as she paced the terrace. "It's because you're a quitter!"

"What are you—"

"You would never have made it with the Red Sox!" Angela snapped. Pausing, she let the words sink in, watching the fire grow in Clay's eyes. "Even if you hadn't been wounded in this war, you'd have found some other excuse—just like you've found one for losing or quitting *all* your jobs."

Clay prepared to strike out at Angela, then he saw tears glistening faintly on her cheeks as she turned away from him.

Angela's voice grew more hushed as she continued to speak. "I'm sorry. It's none of my business what you do with your life." She paused briefly before continuing. "Life is so precious. I've learned that through this war . . . and other things. It just saddens me so to see it wasted."

A solitary crow sailed overhead, silhouetted against the pale sky; its harsh cry rang out across the quiet evening. Beyond the house, the streetlights were winking on one by one.

Angela stood very still for a few moments as though she were waiting to hear her cue in the next line of dialogue. Then she turned toward Clay, saw the emptiness in his face, glanced at the deep shadows beyond him, and hurried up the steps into the house.

Sitting very quietly, Clay tried to assimilate all that Angela had just said, as well as the things she had left unsaid. Now, after she had all but flayed him verbally, he felt for some inexplicable reason closer to her than he had to anyone in his life.

Clay had wanted to get up and take Angela in his arms, kiss her and hold her so close that she would feel like that part of him that he already considered her to be—but he merely sat and sipped his lemonade and watched the last of the rosy light fade into a deep midnight blue.

14

A HELPING HAND

"*F*ive of us and some neighborhood boys on their bicycles. Are we enough to keep the *Journal* going?" Lila lounged on the side of her desk, bumping one foot lazily against it as she spoke.

Henry sat in his chair as erect as a drill sergeant, his hair neatly combed and his black tie knotted tightly. "With a little help from Clay, I can keep the press humming. I won't need him full-time."

"I know I could handle all the commercial and out-of-town deliveries if I just had a truck." Clay sat on the hardwood floor, leaning back against the wall. He wore his Marine combat boots, jeans, and a fatigue shirt.

J.T. stood in the doorway wearing his midsummer outfit, the Harvard sweatshirt with the sleeves cut off and his usual khakis. "I think my old jalopy might do the trick."

"I thought the marshal impounded it a long time ago, J.T." Wearing jeans, a white blouse, and brown penny loafers, Angela sat on the floor next to Clay.

"The judge's order said that *I* can't drive it—didn't say anything about Clay."

"Is that the one parked on the side street next to your office, J.T.?" Lila asked.

"Yep. It's a beauty, ain't it?"

Lila shook her head. "I thought it was an abandoned wreck the town just hadn't gotten around to hauling off."

"Does it run at all, J.T.?" Clay leaned forward, elbows resting on his knees.

"Did when I parked it. At least I *think* it was running. It mighta been towed in. My head was kind of fuzzy that night," J.T. explained. "Now—who knows?"

"Well all it takes is fire and gas to get an engine running if it

175

ain't busted up somewhere." Clay felt encouraged now about the deliveries. "I can handle that part."

Lila gazed around the room at the little group of friends who had gathered to help her save the *Journal*. She felt extremely fortunate in spite of all her problems and realized that she would never trade places with Dobe Jackson. "All right, let's get ourselves organized."

"Take it away, boss lady," J.T. beamed with a quick nod and a wink in Lila's direction.

Lila frowned at him, then continued. "I'll handle the wire services and the government and police beats—they'll have to co-operate with me whether they like me or not since they're public servants."

"If they don't, we'll just put them on the front page. Tell the public they're un-American—trying to sabotage the freedom of the press," J.T. offered with a sly smile. "That's the one thing *all* politicians are afraid of—bad press."

"Will you still take care of the local color articles, J.T.?" Lila asked. "It looks like your idea is becoming the most popular part of the *Journal*."

"Long as Angela keeps typing them." J.T. smiled. "Maybe I oughta just admit it—*writing* them."

"You do all the work, J.T. I just kind of fit it together—like a jigsaw puzzle." Angela smiled.

"Everybody here knows where the *real* work comes in," J.T. admitted, "and since Angela does most of that, I've got plenty of time to sell advertising."

Lila gave him a puzzled look. "I thought you told me you had run out of prospects, J.T."

He scratched his head thoughtfully. "I've been studying on it some since then. Maybe there's a possibility or two that I've over-looked."

"I don't like that gleam in your eyes," Lila admonished. "Just what are you up to?"

"The American way of life, Lila, my love—uh, boss." J.T. cleared his throat, continuing in a more serious vein. "That's what we're fighting this war for, isn't it—democracy and free enterprise, good ol' American ingenuity?"

Lila gave him a level stare over the rim of her glasses. "Just don't do anything that you'd be ashamed of if your mother found out about it."

J.T. thought about that for a moment, rubbing his chin with the knuckle of his forefinger. "Hmm, I think I'd have to stay in bed all day to do that."

"Any other comments?" Lila had to admit that she enjoyed the challenge that lay ahead of her. Dobe Jackson had the power, the money, and the connections, but that just made it all the more interesting.

She thought back to her first days as a fledgling reporter on the Chicago *Tribune* and of how difficult it had been to be taken seriously in a man's world. It had been a long hard fight then, but she had proven herself in the end—and she had done it alone. Now she thought, glancing around the room, *How can I possibly lose when I have friends like these standing with me?*

"I'll be here every day to answer the phone, do the filing and typing—and whatever else you need." Angela had come to feel that Lila was almost like a second mother to her in the months she had been helping out part-time at the office.

Lila merely nodded at Angela, thankful for her friendship and for the changes that she had seen in her life. "Well, if everybody's clear on what they're doing, I guess we'd better get to work. We've got a newspaper to get out."

* * *

"Whadda you mean 'prescription to a newspaper?' I can't even read."

J.T. grinned at the bewildered expression on the sharp, pinched face of Moon Mullins, the local manufacturer and distributor of White Lightning. "It's *sub*scription, Moon, and I don't care whether you read it or not."

Moon perched on a stool in Shorty's Tavern. His whitish hair was slicked back from his low forehead, and his beady eyes and long pointed nose were directed at J.T. "What do I need it for then?"

"So you can do your part to support the war effort," J.T. answered flatly.

Moon tugged at one of his tiny ears and shook his head slowly. "I ain't gettin' this a'tall."

"You can read about the men from Liberty serving in the armed forces. There's an article on one of them in every issue," J.T. explained. "Maybe say a prayer for them."

"Who you kiddin'?" Moon stood up to leave. "I ain't listenin' to no more of this humbug."

As Moon turned toward Shorty, J.T. stared at the back of Moon's head. It looked as though a comb had never touched it although the rest was always slicked down perfectly. Rumor around town had it that Moon was too stupid to know he had hair on the back of his head. "Sit down!"

Surprised at the sharpness of J.T.'s voice, Moon immediately complied.

"Let me pose a question to you, Moon." J.T. frowned at the wail coming from the jukebox as Jimmie Rogers sang one of his songs about loneliness and dying.

"Whut?" Moon asked, his face sullen and sallow-looking in the dim light.

"What do you suppose would happen if the wrong person found out about your," J.T. clasped his hands together, resting his chin on them, "shall we say *clandestine* whiskey business?"

"Clan—whut?"

"Let's say, just for the sake of speculation, that a reporter found out about it and that it made the front page of the newspaper. What do you think would happen?"

"But Dobe . . ."

"I'm not talking about Dobe Jackson." J.T. waved the remark aside. "He'd lose too many of *his* customers if he put you out of business and cut off their supply of hooch."

"Ring wouldn't do nothin' neither," Moon said smugly. "He's in on the whole thing."

"No? I beg to disagree," J.T. said in exaggerated politeness. "I think the good women of Liberty would have our somewhat jaded town marshal tarred and feathered if they found out he was letting you slide because you give him a free bottle now and then. They'd probably do the same thing to anybody else associated with such a shoddy affair. Ring would have you in the calaboose before you could say, 'Still—what still?'"

"Half the town already knows whut's going on," Moon

boasted, grinning slyly at Shorty. "Ain't nobody never done nothin' to stop me yet."

"He's right," Shorty agreed.

"Good point," J.T. admitted, then paused for effect while both men leaned toward him for the finish. "But if it made the papers—the powers that be would *have* to do something about it—and you know it, too."

Moon bared his tiny rodentlike teeth. "This sounds like blackmail to me. I thought that lady that runs the *Journal* was supposed to be such a good Christian woman—churchgoing and all that."

"Oh, she is! Make no doubt about that, Moon," J.T. nodded. "But I'm not!"

"If she's so all-fired righteous how come she ain't done something? It's her newspaper, ain't it?"

"Right again. And if she knew about what you did for a living and how many of Liberty's fair citizens were supporting you, she'd have the whole mess out in the open so fast you wouldn't know what hit you." J.T. stood up, walked over to the jukebox, and unplugged it. The record ground down to a dull growl and stopped.

Moon glanced back at Shorty who shrugged and busied himself rinsing glasses.

"But she *doesn't* know," J.T. continued in the sudden, heavy silence of the tavern as he walked deliberately back over to the bar, "and I don't think you or Ring or a lot of other people want her to find out."

Moon reached into his back pocket and took out his wallet. "How much for one of them prescriptions?"

"It's not quite that simple, Moon."

"Whut?"

"You got forty, maybe fifty regular customers on your route. I think every *one* of 'em needs a *prescription*. All that don't already have one."

"Are you crazy?" Moon glanced over at Shorty as though pleading for help. "I can't make 'em do that!"

"Nothing to it," J.T. grinned. "And since you're such a good friend, I've got it all figured out for you."

Moon lay his head on the edge of the bar, then sat up quickly. "This is the worst day of my life!"

"Oh, come on, Moon," J.T. encouraged. "Think of it as your patriotic duty."

Moon stared at the bright rectangle of the front door as though wishing he could be someplace else.

"All you have to do," J.T. continued in a reassuring voice, "is offer your customers a discount on their whiskey if they'll take the *Journal*. Tell them it's so they can keep up with what's happening with our fighting men from Liberty. Nobody could turn that down—especially when your discount pays for the newspaper."

"That'll ruin me!"

"No it won't, and you know it," J.T. said matter-of-factly, motioning for Shorty to bring him another Coke. "You're making a killing. Besides you can bump the prices up a little in six months or so, and nobody'll know the difference."

Moon stared at the bottle of Coke that Shorty placed on the counter in front of J.T. "That stuff must be doing something bad inside your head, J.T. Never saw a man yet quit drinking and didn't go kindly nuts. Maybe you oughta take it up agin."

"So—how many prescriptions can I count on for you and your customers, Moon?"

"I'll let you know Monday."

"Splendid!" J.T. turned toward Shorty.

"Put me down for one. I'll make Edna read it to me."

*   *   *

After showering, Clay dressed in his faded jeans, white T-shirt and Marine boots with their straps and buckles on the sides. He had always liked their distinctive look, and the boots were the most comfortable footwear he had ever owned. On the way out the door he glanced back at the alarm clock next to his bed. *Midnight—what a time to be going to work!*

Stepping out onto the landing, Clay felt the sultry night air against his skin like a warm, damp cloth. The stars looked hot and white in the sky. Only the moon seemed cold and remote, bathing the world in a bluish light.

Clay stopped in surprise at the bottom of the stairs. Sitting on the back of J.T.'s battered old pickup with her legs dangling over the tailgate, Angela looked dreamlike, her face and bare arms almost luminescent in the pale moonlight.

"What in the world are you doing up?" Clay asked as soon as he found his voice.

"Same as you. Going to work." Angela wearing her work outfit—white tennis shoes, jeans, and a sleeveless cotton blouse—glanced upward. "Isn't this beautiful?"

Clay walked over to the truck. his face dark under the moon. "Angela, I'm afraid you don't know what's in store for you. This is backbreaking work we're talking about."

Angela smiled brightly at him. "You think I'm over the hill at twenty-four?"

"No—you are most *definitely* not over the hill," Clay assured her, glancing at her trim figure. "You're what? Five-three and maybe a hundred and five pounds."

"Close. Maybe you ought to get a job guessing weights at the carnival."

Clay smiled at her. "OK, you win. Let's hope you can keep that sense of humor after tossing those bundles of newspapers around in ninety-five degree heat." He checked the wooden sideframes he had pieced together from scrap lumber and attached to the truck.

They climbed into the cab. Clay touched the starter and the engine roared into life.

"You really do know about engines, don't you?"

"Everybody knows a little something." Clay eased the transmission into first with a clunk. Pulling around from the side of the garage through the portico, he drove down the long driveway to the street.

Angela took a red Thermos bottle from the floorboard, unscrewed the top and poured steaming coffee into a cup. "Here, this ought to get your heart pumping."

Clay took it, sipping the hot coffee carefully. "Mm, that's good! It's strong, but it doesn't have a bite to it—that's a hard formula to come by."

"Eggshells."

"What?"

"I put a spoonful of ground-up eggshell in with the coffee. They cut down on the acid."

Clay leaned on the window ledge with his elbow, letting the

sticky night air cool him as they rode through the quiet, darkened streets. A dog barked in the distance. The streetlights looked misty in the dampness.

"It's got to rain today as hot and sticky as it is already," Clay remarked.

Angela wiped her forehead with a delicate lace-trimmed handkerchief. "I feel like we're riding around underwater."

Noticing the flash of white in Angela's hand, Clay reached down on the floorboard, picked up two fluffy white towels, and dropped them on the seat next to her. "I think you'll find one of these more practical later on."

"I think you're right." Angela took the cup from Clay and sipped the remainder of his coffee. She felt a thrill of excitement at being out in the early darkness, of riding the deserted streets, thinking of all the people still asleep in their beds. It made her feel useful—a necessary part of the town—and important to the lives of the people she worked with. She had longed for this sense of belonging all her life, and the taste of it was like nectar.

Angela glanced over at Clay, who looked relaxed and casual behind the wheel. Somehow he always seemed to maintain that calm exterior even when she knew there was a torrent of emotion raging inside of him. She never failed to notice the tiny crook in his right elbow, thinking of how that slight and barely detectable angle between shoulder and wrist had changed the course of his life.

* * *

"Well, that's the last one." Clay fit the final bale of newspapers securely onto the last stack on the pickup. Tying a rope to the frame, he tossed an end to the other side and started to walk around to secure the papers in place.

"I've got it over here," Angela called out, slipping the rope through the rail and tossing the end back to Clay. "You handle that side."

Clay knew that Angela was already exhausted from helping him load the truck. He had tried to get her to take a break, but she had refused, except to get water. "You keep this up and you might have a real future hauling papers, Mrs. Spain."

Angela's voice was throaty from exertion. "That's not especially funny right now. Why don't you try me after I've had a hot shower and eight hours of sleep?"

"We're just beginning *this* day's fun," Clay taunted. "It's not even three o'clock yet."

Glancing up at the moon's slow drift through its sea of stars, Angela wondered if she had overestimated her endurance. "Don't worry, I'll make it."

After securing the load, Clay vaulted up on the side of the concrete loading dock. Reaching down to Angela, he pulled her up beside him. "You sure you can make it the rest of the day?"

Angela nodded, not wanting to waste her breath.

"Gonna be another hot one!" Henry walked out the open double doors that led onto the dock at the back of the building. As always, with his fresh shave and neatly combed hair, he looked as though he had just stepped out of the shower.

Clay glanced over his shoulder at him, then beyond into the building where the stacked cylinders of newsprint stood in formation like Henry's infantry. "Yep. 'Course it's only three months until October. Don't you ever sleep?"

"On occasion. I try not to make a habit of it though," Henry replied, setting a gallon jug of ice water and two Dixie cups down next to Clay.

"Why come in so early?"

"For one thing, I like to have at least one person around the place all the time. I don't trust our competition to fight fairly." Henry stared off beyond the glare of the loading dock into the night as though expecting an attack. "That Dobe Jackson's got the same gleam in his eyes as Mussolini."

"Oh, come on, Henry," Angela admonished gently. "He can't be *that* bad."

Henry shrugged. "I had to replace some bearings in the press anyway."

"Well, we'd better get on the road." Clay hopped down and offered to help Angela.

She handed him the water jug and cups instead and leaped down herself.

"That's good," Clay encouraged her, walking around to the truck. "I like an independent woman."

"Oh, Clay . . ." Henry called out.

Clay paused, his foot on the truck's running board, the water jug cradled under his arm.

"What time do you think you'll get finished?"

"Oughta be back around ten."

"I'm gonna need your help for two or three hours," Henry said, glancing back into the building at the press, like a mother hen keeping watch over a baby chick.

"Fine."

"You'll still have three or four hours to catch some sleep before you have to be back here to help me with the evening run." Henry grinned. "We don't want you getting bedsores."

"Fat chance."

"And, Angela . . ."

"Yes, Henry, I know," Angela moaned. "Lila needs me to do some typing for her and to try to make some sense out of J.T.'s latest pile of gobbledy-gook."

"Right you are," Henry chirped cheerfully. "I'm so glad we're all volunteers in this outfit."

Angela got through the next few hours on sheer determination. They had visited what seemed to her every business in three counties although they never actually left the Liberty city limits. She felt that she would see shadowed loading ramps and overgrown alleyways in her dreams. She carried bundles of newspapers until her arms ached like fire and felt like lead.

At seven o'clock they finished the town route and headed out into the country. Now the stops would be much farther apart and they'd have time to catch their breath in between them. Angela had never felt so exhausted in her life. She steeled herself for the first stop when she would again slide out of the blessed refuge of the truck seat, take a bundle from Clay after he scrambled up into the truck bed to begin the unloading, and stumble with it to the drop-off point.

They pulled into the graveled parking area in front of Three Corners' Grocery just as the sun climbed above a distant treeline. After leaving three bundles on the benches next to the front door, she climbed wearily back into the truck. Already the air was becoming stifling from the sun's brief appearance.

Clay poured her a cup of water. The remaining ice clinked against the side of the glass jug. "You tired?"

Accepting the water, Angela thought it had the feel of a lead bar as she lifted it to her mouth. "Who me? No, I'm fine. Why do you ask?"

Clay shrugged, started the truck, and pulled out onto the highway. Two minutes later, driving into the red glare of sunlight, he caught a slight movement out of the corner of his eye.

Angela, still holding a half cup of water, had slid quietly down the backrest until her head rested on the seat next to Clay. The water gurgled softly onto the floor of the truck.

Clay gazed at the long dark lashes that curved across the delicate skin beneath her closed eyes. Taking both hands off the steering wheel briefly, he folded the cleanest of the two towels and slipped it beneath her head. With his free hand, he smoothed her hair gently in place.

Three hours later, Angela was still sleeping peacefully as Clay backed the truck up next to the loading ramp behind the *Journal*.

15

A PALE AND SILVER SHINING

"What a day!" Clay pulled the pickup beneath the portico and leaned on the steering wheel with both elbows.

Angela gave him a tired smile. "Think on the bright side. Henry didn't have any work for you and Lila said that I was all caught up, too—for today."

"You're right," Clay yawned. "Now I can sleep six, maybe even seven hours till I have to go back in and help him with the evening's run."

"J.T.'s doing a great job of getting new subscriptions, but it sure makes our route longer." Angela gazed at Clay's clean profile against the midmorning sun that blazed beyond the shadowed portico. She found herself attracted to his humor, his honesty, and the quiet strength of his ways, but she fought against the warmth that stirred inside her each time they were together. Always the shadow of that fatal and unbearable afternoon fell between them. Guilt bound her as securely as chains.

Clay grinned obliquely at Angela, his teeth white against his tanned face. "That rascal's pulling some kind of shenanigans to sell as many newspapers as he is. I don't know what, but I bet you Lila would skin him if she found out."

Angela gazed through the cracked windshield at the periwinkles growing near the far edge of the terrace. Even in the hot August sunshine, they appeared as cool as early frost. "I think these past few weeks have been some of the best times I've had in my whole life."

Caught off guard, Clay leaned back against the torn seat cover without comment, staring at Angela's flushed face, feeling the almost physical presence of her emotion.

"I never had any close friends before." Quickly she turned away and wiped her face with a towel. Then she glanced over at Clay, her eyes shining with simple happiness. "I've even enjoyed running this miserably hot and tiring route with you. I think I just realized it."

Clay cleared his throat. He wanted to tell her that when he awakened in the hot, hard hours of the night when the protean shapes in the darkness closed in on him that a single thought of her always put his mind as ease and sleep once again became his friend. A dozen thoughts swirled in his mind, but he merely said, "You enjoy this?"

"Strangely enough—I do."

Clay couldn't bring himself to admit that the very best time of the day for him was bounding down the stairs at midnight and catching his first glimpse of her waiting for him on the tailgate of the truck. It made him spring from bed with the first ring of the alarm clock and caused him to sing badly and off-key and with unabandoned joy in the shower. "Well, they say simple pleasures are best. This sure isn't complicated."

"But it's fun."

"If you say so."

"Gets you in shape, too," Angela continued espousing the merits of hard work. "After three weeks of this, I feel better than I ever have, that is when I get a chance to rest."

"If I could teach a mule to drive this truck, you'd have another partner real quick."

Angela laughed softly, stretched lazily, and got out of the truck. Then she turned and leaned back through the window. "You want some breakfast?"

"Sure."

"Good. Let's get cleaned up; I'll see you in the kitchen in thirty minutes."

"It's a date." Clay felt uneasy at the sound of the word, but shrugged it off.

After a quick shower and a fifteen-minute rest, Clay put on jeans and a Marine T-shirt. Heading downstairs in his bare feet, he walked over to the house and knocked on the back door.

"It's open."

Entering the dim, shadowy foyer, he walked down the hall to the kitchen.

"Bacon, eggs over easy, toast, fresh-squeezed orange juice, and plenty of hot coffee. How's that sound?" Angela stood in front of the stove lifting bacon out of a large iron skillet with a fork, her face shiny clean from the shower. She had put on a pink cotton blouse, jeans, and white sandals.

Clay poured a cup of coffee from the big pot on the stove and sat down at the table. "No thanks. I'll just have a cold piece of corn pone."

Angela ignored his corny remark, breaking two eggs into the skillet, which popped and hissed.

"Grease is too hot."

"Really. You want to try it?"

Clay got up and crossed to the stove, where he lifted the skillet off the burner and turned the gas down. After allowing the skillet to cool briefly, he set it back down on the fire and splashed grease gently over both eggs until they turned the color of their shells flecked with bits of bacon.

"Not bad. The edges aren't crispy like when I fry them," Angela admitted.

"Learned it doing KP in the Marines." Just the sound of the word *Marines* took the edge off the pleasant sensation Clay had been experiencing by being with Angela.

Clay finished the cooking and put the food on the table. As they ate at the long table in the shadowed kitchen, he fought against the memories that had surfaced unbidden and unwanted.

Overhead the wooden blades of a fan hanging down from the high ceiling circled slowly, stirring the warm air. Their conversation had slowed down to a trickle and then dried up completely. Down the long hallway a grandfather clock ticked off the minutes with polished precision.

Almost without warning, a thunderhead rolled up from the south, darkening the air as the temperature dropped fifteen degrees in five minutes. Through the tall windows, a white web of lightning flashed against a black wall of clouds. A peal of thunder rolled over the house like a wave of sound, rattling the glass panes in their hardwood frames.

Angela dropped her fork on the plate, jumped up, and ran

over to the open window. In the wind, the long curtains were streaming into the room. "Oh, this is so beautiful!"

Clay watched Angela's hair blow wildly about her face and shoulders. The air seemed charged with the full force of the electrical storm.

Angela sensed Clay's presence before he touched her. Then she felt his lips brushing gently against the pale curve of her neck as he lifted the soft dark mass of hair aside. She remained motionless before the open window as the wind blew a fine cool mist against the warm skin of her face.

Turning to him, Angela lifted up on tiptoe as he kissed her gently, his hand cradling the small of her back. She circled his lean waist with her arms, lost in the urgent demand of his lips. Suddenly a bolt of lighting, popping like the sharp crack of a rifle, snapped off an oak limb. It crashed down with a heavy crunching sound just outside the window.

Angela pulled away, breathless in the sweep of the storm, still lost in the sudden wonder of their embrace. She stared out at the storm, at the gray and misty sheet of rain moving across the wide lawn toward them. Torn between passion and her newfound faith, she trembled before the fury of the storm that raged without and the one that raged within. Even after the miracle of that snowy Christmas in Ollie's Drugstore, she felt burdened by a guilt so dark and heavy that she had told no one about it, but it gnawed at her peace of mind like a furtive rodent.

Taking Clay's hand, Angela felt its strength and its tenderness. She ran her fingertips along a vein that traveled the back of his hand from the knuckle of his ringfinger to the wrist. Without speaking or looking into his face, she turned quickly and left the kitchen, running down the long hall toward her bedroom.

Clay remained at the window, listening to the rain pound flatly on the stone terrace and rush in torrents down the metal gutters. He walked to the hallway and stared after Angela. Then he let himself out through the back door into the cool driving rain.

* * *

In the long refreshing shadows of late afternoon, Angela sat on the terrace. A tall glass of iced tea made a wet ring on the marble-topped table beside her. The storm had left the town wet and glistening in the late sunlight. Leaves and tree limbs lay scattered across the property.

Angela watched a blue jay, its wings glinting like cobalt in the last slanting rays of sunlight, lift from a low branch and sail out of sight beyond the high eaves of the house. She picked up her glass and took a small sip, savoring the sweet, comforting flavor of the iced tea, which she associated with many of her good memories. For half an hour she had been glancing every minute or two at the empty stairs leading up to the garage apartment.

"My, that certainly looks refreshing!" Lila remarked as she came around the corner of the house. Wearing a tan suit and white blouse, she looked the picture of the successful businesswoman.

"It surely is. Here have some." Angela poured her a glass of tea.

Lila glanced at the extra glass near the chair across from Angela. "You're not expecting someone are you?"

Angela couldn't stop herself from taking a quick look at the stairs. "No."

Sitting down, Lila surveyed the littered yard. "That storm made a mess, didn't it?"

"Oh, Amos will have it cleaned up in no time. He's the best worker I know," Angela paused briefly, her eyes growing suddenly dark, "except for Clay."

"He does earn a day's pay, doesn't he?" Lila agreed. "By the way, where is he? I'm surprised he's not having a little refreshment out here with you before he has to go back and help Henry get tonight's run going."

"Resting, I suppose."

"Are you two getting along all right?"

Angela glanced again at the stairs. "Oh, sure. We get along just fine."

"Well, if you don't, you're certainly putting on a good act every time I see you together." Lila could see the uneasiness in Angela's manner but didn't want to interfere with her private life. "You actually seem to enjoy all the hard work."

"I do."

Angela glanced up at Lila, then took a swallow of her drink. "It's so beautiful after the storm. The whole world looks so clean and smells so fresh."

Lila gazed out at the shining wet trees and flowers. "You can almost understand why God destroyed the world once with water. I'm sure the whole earth must have looked brand new after the flood subsided."

Angela nodded, making circles of water on the tabletop with the bottom of her glass.

Lila decided that Angela needed to talk about something, but that she was having difficulty admitting it, even to herself. "Is there something I can do for you, Angela? You seem to have something on your mind."

"Oh, I don't know. Maybe it's the way I'll always be." Angela pushed the glass away from her.

"Is it Clay?"

Angela lifted her eyes, a lingering sadness in their depths. "No, Clay's fine."

"The last thing I want to do is interfere in your life. If I can't help you, I certainly don't want to do anything that would upset you."

Angela knew that Lila respected her privacy. She also knew that she could confide in her, and she suddenly felt the need to do just that.

"Sometimes it helps to talk, but not always. Maybe you'd rather be alone."

"No!" Angela blurted out. "I've been alone quite enough in my life."

Lila sipped her tea, gazing at a fleecy line of clouds just above the horizon. The westering sun had touched their edges with the color of ripe peaches.

"I . . ." Angela started to speak, but couldn't seem to go on. "It's hard to explain."

Lila knew the words would come, and determined that she would put no pressure on Angela.

"I'm a Christian now and I have a peace that could only come from God. But I can't forget what I was in the past, all the times that I . . ."

Lila gave Angela a reassuring nod as Angela glanced up at her, brushing her hair back from her face.

"That afternoon in that awful place when Morton—sometimes I go for a day or two without thinking of it, but it always comes back—especially right before I go to bed." Angela took a swallow of tea, and continued, her voice calmer now. "But after I pray, I just drift right off to sleep."

Lila thought she understood Angela's problem. "Angela, you came under conviction when you accepted Jesus Christ as your Savior. That's why you felt sorry for the things you had done wrong. *That* comes from the Holy Spirit."

"That seems to be just about the way I remember it," Angela nodded with interest.

"But what you're feeling now is guilt about things that you've already confessed, about things that you've already been forgiven for. And that guilt does *not* come from God."

Angela listened attentively, leaning forward on the edge of her chair.

"What you're feeling is just a pack of lies that the devil is telling you to try and tear apart your faith, to rob you of the peace and joy of your new life," Lila continued. "The Bible tells us that Jesus washed us from our sins in his own blood. As far as God is concerned they're gone. So why should *you* worry yourself about them?"

A smile had gradually brightened Angela's face as Lila spoke to her. "You're exactly right. Why *should* I worry?"

"I know it must be especially painful to you when you're around Clay."

Angela nodded.

"You don't have to carry this burden around any longer, Angela."

A bright tear ran quickly down Angela's cheek. She wiped it away, still smiling.

"Just lay it at the foot of the cross."

"I will," Angela whispered.

Lila found as always that when she shared her faith it made her spirit lift within her. "I always like to listen to what Jesus has to say about whatever it is that's bothering us."

Angela felt the heaviness of her guilt lifting as though a weight were being taken off her heart.

Closing her eyes, Lila spoke in a voice that was clear and strong and lilting, "'Come unto me, all ye that labour and are heavy laden, and I will give you rest. Take my yoke upon you, and learn of me; for I am meek and lowly in heart: and ye shall find rest unto your souls.'"

Angela could almost see Jesus in his coarse robes and dusty sandals on a rocky hillside in Galilee, speaking to the multitude of fishermen and farmers and shepherds. Mothers called their children from play, settling them down with the family as they listened to this man who spoke as no man ever had.

Lila, opening her eyes, gazed serenely at Angela. "And then Jesus said, 'For my yoke is easy, and my burden is light.' And it is, it surely is."

The two women sat together, speaking quietly, sharing the ineffable joy of their faith. Then Lila stood up, laying one hand against Angela's forehead and raising the other toward the darkening sky. After a moment Angela stood up. The two of them embraced quickly before Lila walked away down the sidewalk that led around the house.

Ten minutes later, Clay bounded down the steps and ran to the truck.

"Clay . . ."

With his hand on the door, Clay paused. "What is it? I'm running late now."

Angela poured her glass full of tea, added a few half-melted ice cubes, and took it over to the truck. "Thought you might be a little thirsty."

Clay took the tea quickly, drinking half of it without taking the glass from his mouth. "Mm . . . that's just what I needed." He finished the cool liquid and handed the glass back to Angela.

Without any warning, Angela put her arms around his neck and kissed him firmly on the mouth. Pulling away, she smiled up at him. "I thought you might like that, too."

Clay's eyes were wide with surprise; the glass dangled limply in his outstretched hand. "What was that for?"

"Because I enjoyed it."

"But I thought . . ."

Angela took the glass from his hand. "You'd better hurry. Henry's waiting."

"Oh, yeah." Thoroughly confused, Clay slid into the truck and banged the door shut.

"What time do you think you'll be finished tonight?" Angela walked around to the other side of the truck and sat down on the stairs.

"Shouldn't be too long," Clay replied, hardly knowing what to expect next.

"Could you give me a time please?"

"Eight-thirty."

"Good. I don't want the steaks to get cold," Angela smiled wistfully.

"Steaks?"

"You do like porterhouse, don't you?"

"Well, sure, but—"

"Don't be late then."

* * *

The bleachers carried a faint smell of popcorn, chewing gum, and spilled Cokes from the summer baseball season. The storm seemed to have washed the sky so clean that the stars sparkled with a newfound brilliance. With the approach of September, the smell of sweet olive had disappeared from the air, but it lingered still in Clay's memory.

"You aren't much on egg frying, but you sure know what to do with a steak. I'm full as a tick." Clay sat on the second-to-last bleacher, leaning back on his elbows.

Next to him, Angela propped her feet on the weathered plank in front of her, watching the moon rise behind several thin strands of cloud. In its pale and silver shining, they took on the appearance of winter frost.

"Did you hear me?"

Angela turned. "You ate all of yours and half of mine—that's compliment enough."

"I guess it is at that," Clay grinned.

Angela returned to her cloud watching.

Clay leaned forward and took Angela's small hand. His own, hard and tanned, almost completely covered it. "I'm glad you told me about your talk with Lila."

"I am, too," Angela replied softly, still staring out into the night sky.

Clay felt a tenderness toward Angela that he never would have imagined himself capable of. He wanted to spend the rest of his life with her, to keep her safe, to wake each morning and see her next to him. "I didn't mean to upset you this morning in the kitchen, Angela. I just . . ."

Angela patted the top of his hand, then rubbed it gently, feeling the soft texture of the fine sun-bleached hair against her fingertips.

"I hope things are all right between us now."

"It wasn't your fault at all, Clay," Angela assured him, "and things are just fine between us."

Feeling awkward, Clay had no words to express the emotion that rose in his chest. It was almost like the tingling excitement he felt before he walked out to the pitcher's mound at the beginning of a game, but stronger and more enduring. He thought that nothing could ever change it, that Angela must surely feel it pulsing through his hand.

"I'm glad things are going well at the *Journal*," Clay finally said, "for Lila's sake."

In the moonlight, Angela's face looked as placid as the surface of a still woodland pool. "I am too. As hard as she's worked, she surely deserves it."

Clay suddenly realized what Angela had meant about actually enjoying all the hard work. All his life, work had been something necessary, something that was expected and required. It was how you got what you wanted out of life. But somehow the past few weeks had been much different and he finally saw it. "You know you're right."

"About what?"

"About all this hard work we've been doing," Clay continued. "It is fun!"

Angela gave the moon a thoughtful glance. "I think it's because we're almost like a little family—the five of us."

"I think you're right. Even when I was pitching, I don't think I really enjoyed the *game*. I was always thinking of what I could get for myself if I worked hard enough: money, a big expensive car, my name in the newspapers."

"Maybe the difference is who you're working for," Angela suggested.

"And who I'm working *with*," Clay added. He gazed out at the darkened baseball diamond. "Maybe I won't miss it nearly as much as I thought I would."

Angela leaned against him as they sat alone in the bleachers in the silver moonlight.

16

CLOSE TO THE HEART

"Nothing like a good piece of hickory." J.T. twisted the ax handle in both hands, feeling the balance and the smoothly sanded texture of the wood.

Clay sat on the floor, leaning back against a cool steel beam just inside the doors that led to the loading dock. He tapped the end of his bat once on the concrete floor. "You're wrong there, Counselor. Nothing beats ash."

"Well, I hope we don't get the chance to find out which one's best tonight," J.T. admitted.

"You really think they'll come?"

"Who knows?" J.T. stood up and gazed out a back window, sparkling clean thanks to Lila's constant attention to the building.

"Well, if they don't show up tonight, then they won't show at all," Clay muttered. "They know this is the only night the press isn't running."

J.T. glanced at his watch in the anemic light from the window, then sat back down. "I don't usually put much stock in what Shorty picks up from that bunch of pulpwood haulers and out-of-work gas-station attendants that hang around his place, but he said this was the real thing."

"How does he know what the 'real thing' is?" Clay had no confidence at all in the crew from Shorty's, having been one of them himself in the past.

"Volume, I believe," J.T. explained briefly. "Said that *everybody* seemed to know about it."

"Maybe somebody went on a recruiting campaign there," Clay ventured. "Shorty's would be a likely place to find men looking for a quick buck for thirty minutes' work. There's a lot of traffic up and down that highway, men just passing through on their way to who knows where."

* * *

They came at one-thirty-eight. J.T. heard a muffled curse as one of them stumbled over something at the foot of the loading dock. He glanced over at Clay who was dozing, his head slumped down on his shoulder.

J.T. put his hand over Clay's mouth. He motioned for him to be quiet when he awakened with a start, then pointed toward the outside. Clay nodded and stood up.

Easing over to the window, J.T. peered out. In the deep shadows cast by a feeble bulb that hung from a long cord over the loading dock, he saw the three men, dressed in heavy coats with felt hats pulled low over their faces. They lurked near the ramp as though planning their course of action. Then they walked cautiously toward the back door, glancing furtively about. One was a tall brute of a man, the other two short—one slim and the other stocky. All three carried sledgehammers over their shoulders.

J.T. and Clay positioned themselves on either side of the door. Outside, a bolt cutter snapped through the padlock. The door opened slowly, letting a narrow beam of light into the murky darkness. The stocky man appeared first, glancing from side to side then entering the room silently followed by the slim one. Both moved slowly toward the printing press.

Waving Clay off, J.T. shouldered his ax handle. As the big man took his first step inside, J.T. swung the ax handle as hard as he could, cutting the man's legs out from under him. With a terrible roar he landed heavily on the concrete floor. Sprawled in the long, thin rectangle of light, he turned over quickly, his sledgehammer raised above his head.

Clay's bat crashed down on the man's right hand, crushing it with a sound like twigs snapping. The hammer rattled into the darkness as the man bellowed in pain.

J.T. had already turned toward the other two who stood frozen at the edge of the light. Leaving the big man on the floor, writhing and moaning in pain, Clay joined J.T., fanning out to his left in a flanking movement.

The two men, jerking their heads in every direction now looking for a way out, knew their situation as well as J.T. and Clay did. The heavy sledgehammers were perfect for demolishing the printing press but were far too clumsy to wield in hand-to-hand combat against their two opponents who now faced them holding lighter weapons.

In desperation, the stocky man charged Clay, swinging his hammer in a roundhouse motion. Clay easily sidestepped the blow as the hammer swished past his head then slammed his bat against the man's back as he went by. His breath went out of him in a rush as the blow sent him skittering across the concrete floor where he lay gasping for air.

Twenty-five feet away, J.T., holding his ax handle loosely in front of his chest, closed in on the third man.

Suddenly the door to the front office swung open, sending a glare of light into the darkness. Henry stood in front of the opening, squinting through his glasses at the shadowy figures in the cavernous room.

Seeing his only means of escaping the fate of his two fellows, the third man rushed for the lighted door, his heavy hammer held high.

"Get out of his way!" J.T. yelled at Henry. "Let him get past you!"

Confused as well as protective of his printing press, Henry stepped forward in an effort to stop the man. In doing so the neat little printer from Chicago wrote his own epitaph.

The heavy hammer crushed through the layer of bone above Henry's left ear as if it were an eggshell. He crumpled instantly to the floor as the man threw the hammer into the darkness and flashed through the open door to the lighted reception area and out the front door.

J.T. dropped to Henry's side, lifted his head in his arms then looked away, his face ashen.

Clay stood above them. "Is he . . . ?"

J.T.'s expression answered the question.

A frenzy of memories flashed through Clay's mind—of the nights he and Henry had spent running the press for the next day's edition. He pictured the man's intensity as he huddled over his machine.

In a rage, Clay raced out of the building, looking for the man who had robbed him of a friend. He searched several yards and ran to the end of the block, but he had vanished into the darkness.

When Clay returned, he saw J.T. still sitting on the floor, cradling Henry's head in his lap. The other two men, battered by ax handle and bat, had made their escape unnoticed.

*   *   *

"Remember the time Henry had the press all ready to run the morning edition, and I told him I forgot about picking up those last ten rolls of newsprint down at the depot?" Wearing his black suit with his tie loosened, Clay sat on the couch next to Angela in her huge living room. "You know how he thought the world would end if those papers were a *minute* late coming off the press. I never saw him so mad."

Angela slipped her high heels off and folded her legs under her on the couch, remembering that day, in a time of remembrance the four of them were now sharing. "I never will forget that. Henry picked up a wrench and chased you all the way out to the back fence before you finally showed him those rolls of newsprint in the back of the pickup."

Sipping her coffee from a thin, gold-rimmed cup, Lila spoke in a voice that was little more than a whisper. "If it hadn't been for Henry, I never would have made it with the *Tribune.* He'd come up to the newsroom almost every day to show me the ropes. He'd been with the paper so long, he knew the business inside out. But seeing the finished product rolling off those big presses—that was his one great love."

"What are we gonna do about Dobe Jackson?" J.T. stood at one of the tall windows, watching a mockingbird dive like a fighter plane at a gray squirrel who had climbed the wrong tree. "We *can't* just let him get away with this."

After a momentary silence, Angela spoke for the three of them. "We have to let the law handle it, J.T."

"The law! You mean Ring Clampett?" J.T. turned from the

window, his eyes narrowed in anger. "Ring couldn't find a chicken in a henhouse with a book of instructions. How's he going to find the men who murdered Henry? And that's the *only* way we'll nail Jackson—through them."

"I'm not so sure we could tie him to it even if they *were* caught." Lila turned toward J.T., motioning for him to come sit beside her.

J.T. walked over almost obediently and sat down on the sofa next to her.

"It's an imperfect world, J.T., even in our justice system. But you know that better than any of us." Lila put her hand on his shoulder. "Dobe Jackson's too smart to let himself be directly connected to men like *those* three."

"We all know he was behind it though. He was the only one with a motive." J.T. insisted, his voice rising in anger. "The whole town knows."

"Exactly," Lila said in a level voice.

Angela noticed the portent in Lila's tone. "What are you getting at, Lila?"

"I think the *town's* going to take care of Dobe Jackson," Lila explained. "Oh, they're not going to lock him up or strap him into the electric chair, but a kind of justice *will* be served. I have that much confidence in the people of Liberty."

Clay sat forward on the edge of the sofa. "I still don't understand what you mean."

"It's beginning already." Lila stared at a painting on the opposite wall. It depicted an old man in rough clothes who carried an obviously full bucket up a winding hillside path toward a cabin nestled in the trees. For some reason he reminded her of Henry.

"What's beginning?" J.T. blurted out, growing impatient with Lila's enigmatic answers.

"The supervisor of the *Herald*'s printroom called me about a job."

"He's been there since Jackson took over the newspaper," J.T. remarked in total surprise. "What did you tell him?"

"I told him he had a job."

"That's great!" Clay added. "Now we can keep the press rolling right along."

"You're starting to sound like Henry," Angela grinned.

"Some of the others have called, too." Lila added, still staring at the painting.

J.T. motioned toward Lila with his hand and his head. "They called and . . ."

"I can hire one or two more," Lila continued. "Another reporter maybe and someone to help with the deliveries since Clay's going to be the senior man in the printing section now. But we'll really have to expand to put on many more people."

"Anything else?" J.T. asked.

Angela placed her cup back in the saucer with a soft tinkling sound. "I heard a few people at the funeral say they're canceling their subscriptions to the *Herald*."

"I heard the same thing," J.T. added, "but I didn't think much about it."

"Me, too," Clay put in. "Maybe the town *will* punish Dobe."

"Dobe's had his own way around here for a long time now." J.T. stared at the painting of the old man carrying his bucket. "I guess maybe ordinary people *can* make a difference—if they get a belly full of somebody—and if they stick together."

"I'm speaking almost as an outsider," Lila observed solemnly. "But maybe in a way that gives me an advantage over the three of you. This town's got its share of villains just like every other town, I suppose, but for some reason, I've got confidence that when it comes to something important, like fighting a war against Hitler or uniting against *another* tyrant like Dobe Jackson, the people of Liberty will take charge and put them *both* out of business."

"Can I back up just a little, Lila?" Clay asked, a slight frown on his face.

"Surely."

"Did I hear you say I'd be the senior man in the printing section?"

"That's right," Lila nodded. "The man from the *Herald* will be your assistant."

"But he knows ten times as much as I do about the newspaper business."

"Doesn't matter. You've got seniority on him and you're learning quickly." Lila smiled at Angela. "I've got a feeling that it'll only be a temporary position anyway. If what's happened already is any indication, you'll rise beyond the printing part of the business before long. Just in these last few minutes it seems like I can already see what's going to happen with the *Journal*."

"And what's that?" J.T. asked.

"I just think it's going to grow so fast that none of us will be able to believe it," Lila went on, her face glowing with excitement. "I think Liberty's been ready for a change for a long time now and this last business with Dobe was the final straw."

"A few people quitting, a few more canceling subscriptions . . . I don't recall anything astounding we discussed that would make you believe the *Journal*'s going to take off." J.T. thought Lila had begun to fantasize a little.

"No," Lila agreed, "but I just remembered something I saw at the funeral that makes me *know* it."

J.T. glanced over at Angela and Clay. "You want to let the rest of us in on it, or should we go home and wait for a vision like you had?"

"It wasn't a vision at all," Lila smiled. "But it's a sign almost as certain."

Clay looked at J.T. and shrugged.

"Senator Demerie ignored Dobe Jackson at the funeral today—acted like he didn't even exist."

"Come to think of it, I saw him turn around and walk off when Jackson tried to speak to him," Angela added. "I thought that was kind of strange since he's always been one of the senator's biggest supporters."

"Tyson Demerie is an old-line politician. He's a human weathervane for political winds," Lila explained, staring directly at J.T. "He can smell political *or* economic death on a man like a hyena smells physical death. And for him to treat his biggest contributor in this whole town like he treated Dobe Jackson today, he knows the end is close."

J.T. nodded in agreement. "I don't know why I didn't figure that out myself. Well, even if ol' Dobe has to shut down or sell out, he's got enough money to live like a king for the rest of his life."

"I'm sure that's true," Lila agreed. "Whatever happens though, we're in for some interesting times ahead."

"I can't wait to get back to work," Angela put in. "This is all so exciting!"

In spite of the funeral, Lila felt cheered by Angela's enthusiasm and by the friendship she shared with those who had come together to mourn and remember. "Well, I'm going home to bed. We've go to get the press rolling again tomorrow. The town might overlook one day without a newspaper as a memorial to Henry, but not two days."

After Lila and J.T. had gone, Angela sat next to Clay in front of the tall windows, watching the slanting sunlight fade as purple twilight settled about the town.

Finally Angela broke the silence. "You think you'll keep working at the *Journal?*"

Clay continued to stare out the window, absorbed by the changing colors of the light, remembering the fiery sunsets of the South Pacific. "Probably," he muttered. "Maybe you haven't noticed, but people haven't exactly been standing in line with job offers for me."

"I like working there."

"I know you do." Clay glanced at Angela. "You certainly don't need the money."

"I think there's a real future for you at the *Journal,* Clay. If what Lila was talking about happens, you might take over for her as editor in a year or two. Then she'll be able to spend all her time looking after the business end."

"Maybe. It would sure take some doing to train me as an editor though." Clay replied, taking Angela's hand. "But, whatever happens, I'm glad we've had this time together. Nothing like doing some hard work with a person if you really want to get to know them."

Angela made tiny figure eights on the top of Clay's hand with her fingertip. "Clay . . ."

His eyes narrowed in concern at the tone of Angela's voice. "Something bothering you?"

"If you don't want to talk about it let me know, but sometimes I worry about you."

"Why?"

"It's just that—well sometimes you act like you're off somewhere else, even when you're right here next to me."

Clay felt that Angela knew him better than he had thought. "That's the way I feel sometimes."

Angela squeezed his hand, leaning her head against his shoulder.

"It's almost like I'm living in two places at once," Clay went on, his eyes gazing off into some unknown terrain that only he could see. "When I wake up in the morning I don't know if I'll be here in Liberty or off somewhere in the South Pacific."

The expansive living room was full of shadows now as dusk gave way to night. Out in the hall the grandfather clock punctuated the silence with its metronomic ticking.

After a few moments, Clay continued, speaking as though he were feeling his way through a minefield. "I feel like half a man a lot of the time—like I've only got half a body and half a mind. I can almost see another Clayton McCain still digging into the sand behind a coconut log, trying to get away from the machine gun bullets and the mortars and the artillery."

Angela sat with Clay in the darkness, allowing him to talk it all out, to take some of the pain out of the memories by sharing them with someone else. When he had finished, she kissed him lightly on the cheek. "If it's any comfort to you, Clay, I want you to know that I'll be right here with you—for as long as you want."

Clay leaned forward, rubbing his eyes with both hands. Then he took Angela's hands and kissed her tenderly on the lips. "I think maybe that's enough."

Angela knew that it wasn't, but she also realized that it was something he had to find out for himself.

*　*　*

"'And him that cometh to me I will in no wise cast out.' Jesus first spoke those words almost two thousand years ago, and they're just as real, just as true today as they were then." As the choir rose to stand behind him, Thad Majors closed his Bible and placed it on the pulpit, stepped down from the platform, and stood in front of his congregation. Beaming his crinkly, genuine smile at his church, he extended his arms. "Come to Jesus. A million years from now you'll still be rejoicing in this day."

> Just as I am, without one plea,
> But that Thy blood was shed for me,
> And that Thou bidd'st me come to Thee,
> O Lamb of God, I come! I come!

Angela knew this was Clay's hour. She had seen it coming for some time now and had been with him at two o'clock this same morning when he had made the decision to give his life to Jesus Christ. She smiled back at him as he patted her hand and rose from the pew. Her eyes shining with tears, she watched him walk purposefully down the aisle of the church toward Majors, who stood waiting like a proud bridegroom.

Majors shook Clay's hand and spoke with him a few minutes, tilting his head forward so he could hear above the singing. Then he introduced him to the church, telling them of Clay's decision. With heartfelt "amens" the church accepted him as a member, then passed by in a long line to welcome him into the church.

As she always would at such times, Angela recalled that bitter cold and snowy Christmas Eve at Ollie's when she had finally seen the light shining in darkness. The noonday sunshine streamed in through the tall stained-glass windows, bathing the church in a rainbow of colors, but Angela saw only Clay's face shining with the joy of a brand-new life.

Angela also knew that something else lay close to the heart of Clay McCain. As they walked the shady sidewalks of Liberty toward home together after the service, he spoke it aloud.

"Angela, there's something I've been wanting to talk to you about," Clay began, as nervous as a boy holding a bat in front of a broken window.

"Yes?" Angela determined that she would enjoy every second of it.

"I don't really know how to begin," Clay mumbled, kicking a fallen twig off the sidewalk.

Angela waved at Ora Peabody, who passed them on the other side of the street. "Offhand, I'd say you should just start right at the beginning."

"Well, it's just that—"

"Yes."

"What?"

"Yes. Oh, for goodness sake, Clay! Yes, I'll marry you." Angela turned to him and, on tiptoe, kissed him full on the lips. "Now, is there anything else?"

Dazed, Clay stared down at her. "You mean you really want to marry me?"

"No, I don't think it's that actually." Angela pursed her lips in mock concentration. "I'm just tired of waiting for you to come down the stairs of that garage apartment every morning, and this is the only way I see out of it."

Clay grinned and took her hand as they continued down the sidewalk. April had come again and with it the fragrance of the sweet olive blossoms. The memories came back, too, and the dreams of glory, but Clay no longer felt the pain. Putting his arm around Angela's waist, he pictured a giant stadium and a young man who looked very much like him on the mound. He saw the familiar windup and the blazing fastball as the last batter went down.